LINDSEY N. RHODEN

DECEPTION, DEATH & THE DIVINE

For anyone trying to find their own strength in the midst of the
breaking.

CONTENT WARNING

Deception, Death, And The Divine is an **adult** dark fantasy novella meant for an 18+ audience. This novella contains scenes of graphic violence, shadow play, light bondage, light choking, attempted sexual assault and animal death on page. Some of this content may be triggering to individuals and should be taken into account before reading.

Playlist

- ▶ **GOD NEEDS THE DEVIL**
  JONAH KAGEN

- ▶ **THE FRUITS**
  PARIS PALOMA

- ▶ **PLAY WITH FIRE**
  SAM TINNESZ, YACHT MONEY

- ▶ **DEVIL'S BACKBONE**
  THE CIVIL WARS

- ▶ **DEITY**
  VALEREE

- ▶ **BAD FOR YOU**
  CHAPPEL ROAN

- ▶ **LIKE YOU MEAN IT**
  STEVEN RODRIGUEZ

- ▶ **HOW VILLAINS ARE MADE**
  MADALEN DUKE

- ▶ **O'DEATH - HAUNTED VERSION**
  BOBBY BASS, LAURA PALEY, COLM R. MCGUINNES

From the archives of the Keepers of Time, Wisdom and Destiny.

There are moments in time where even we cannot predict how dark things will become. All we can say is we regret the things that were asked of us, the depth of the darkness we had to find in order to reclaim peace for this world. It was too high a price to pay. And for that, we will do whatever is necessary to ensure that peace remains. As a testament and reminder of the price that was paid, we've collected and arranged a firsthand account of our sins against the Deities, may they rest in peace. Let this story live as a reminder of the blood that was shed and the sacrifices made.

May we never have to relive that darkness.

The story of Death and the Divine.

CHAPTER 1
The Divine

The daylight dancing through the garden just outside the palace window was calling me. Despite Arne's insistence for an urgent council meeting, I found myself wandering through the palace to soak in every last moment of peace I could before I was called to my duties. Working with the others, the very political nature of it all—it had never been my strong suit. But at least beneath the rays of sunlight amidst the Realm of the Gods, I could always find some comfort.

As I made my way past the council chamber and into the gardens, I relished in the safety of our home, the peace and joy that I'd spent so long cultivating alongside my counterparts. It wasn't perfect by any means, but it was the only home I knew.

We reigned together, an equal council of rulers overseeing the mortal realms and the magical ones full of fae rulers and mystical creatures. Despite our positions of equality, there were still power plays and political nonsense to put up with. I had no interest in that, in ruling or power or any of the other fleeting things they bothered themselves with. There was enough distrust and scheming amongst the deities to last our lifetime, and I felt my time was better spent separate from all of that. I just wanted to exist amidst my creation, watching it thrive and ensuring its safety.

I'd finally started to manifest that here, despite the constant discord and growing unrest amongst the realms. I'd always felt like something of an outsider amongst the other deities. My power was different, stronger than any of theirs, but with only one purpose. The others could control certain elements within the realms: love, power, the outcome of battles, and so on. But my magic was the only one with the ability to create something out of nothing, to breathe life into nothingness. It was a power the others didn't understand and it kept them on guard, constantly questioning and watching.

My mind eased as I strode into the gardens, the world beyond melting away as I greeted my creations. I breathed deeply, the plant life around me reaching up in unison with my own breath. Not many understood or acknowledged the life that existed within even the smallest stem. It wasn't at all unlike the life that existed within the fae, the mortals, even the animals that walked their realms. It was *all* life in my eyes, all tender beings brought forth by my magic, therefore making me responsible to look after it.

I knelt beside a new patch of dirt. Golden light swirled in the air as I stretched out my fingers and bade the ground to make way for the peonies breaking forth. Specks of bright green broke through, unfurling as the stalks grew taller to reveal the small blush colored blossoms within its folds. I stood, a smile stretching across my face as I watched my latest addition. It was nearly impossible to resist the urge to add a little inflorescence here and there on my afternoon walks through the gardens. Seeing the new blossoms coming to life and opening beneath my power was one of life's simple joys—a small fraction of my magic, yet something that still made me smile after all this time.

The smile was short-lived as I watched the newly blooming peonies shrink away, wilted and withered within a mere matter of seconds. A mist as dark as obsidian settled over the gardens, darkness and shadow swallowing everything within reach.

I bit down, locking my jaw as I felt a familiar rush of irritation.

"What are you doing here, Death?" I asked without turning around to acknowledge him. Death was the only one of the deities who didn't reside in the palace full time. It was a small mercy—a much appreciated one on my account, due to the contrast in our abilities. Being in the presence of utter destruction when my sole purpose was to create proved to be rather frightening. His power clashed with mine, its essence reaching through the air and causing my blood to chill. His shadows were all consuming, striking fear to my very core. I could practically feel the creeping tendrils of icy obsidian clawing to get closer, straining to cling on to the warm, golden glow of my own magic.

He sauntered up beside me, eyeing the now dead peonies with an arrogant smirk.

In our endless years together, his demeanor had never changed—always the same hardened cold. His hair mimicked the endless black of night, slicked back and cascading down his shoulders in silken strands, contrasting against the deep hollows of his face and the pale sheen of his skin, which had always reminded me of a skull.

He was dressed head to toe in his usual black, the cut of his tunic fitting tightly around his arms, with a black silk vest he must have added as a touch of flare for this meeting. His pants were cut in the same trim manner, emphasizing the finely cut silhouette of his body and leaving little to the imagination.

"What a pity," he mocked as he turned away from the flowers to face me. "Really, Caili, why must you still be so formal with me? Even after all this time."

I huffed, gathering my skirts in one hand to sidestep him and return to my walk.

"That is not my name. It would do you good to learn a bit of formality and respect in my presence, Death. You may refer to me as Cailleach or the Divine." I shot him a look over my shoulder, hoping my features didn't betray the fear I felt coursing through my body. "Nothing else."

I watched the wicked grin that spread across his face, knowing he'd hit a nerve as he always did when he used that irritating nickname. I hated how easily he played me, how he delighted in my vexation. I tried to avoid interactions with him, tried to let Arne handle things with the god of the underworld. The other deities had agreed, insisting Death was far too unstable to trust.

I rolled my eyes, letting a huff of frustration slip between my lips as I turned away once more and continued my walk through the gardens.

"The others have called for a meeting," he called out finally, a twinge of annoyance in his tone.

I reached out to the hedges along my path, running my fingers through the dark green leaves as Death followed in my wake. "I'm surprised you could tear yourself away from your duties long enough to grace us with your presence." It was no big secret amidst the Realm of the Gods how Death preoccupied himself. "Whatever will the realms do without you on the prowl, hunting innocents?"

"As much as I do enjoy the consumption of wayward souls, I am well aware that my responsibilities don't end there." He paused, causing my steps to slow as I waited for him to speak whatever thoughts were stirring in his mind. "And I promise you, Cailli, they are not all as innocent as you assume they are."

I spun on him, fear making way for anger as I spat his venom back in his face for speaking of the death of my creation so indifferently. "You consume my creation, corrupt it, and claim it for that death pit you call a home. And you have the audacity to stand here and tell me they deserve it?" My words shook with pent-up rage from centuries of violence bestowed upon my creation at his hands.

Death's expression hardened, his lips pursing as he refused to answer. I scoffed, turning back to my path and busying myself with the maintenance of a rosebush. Even with his mist choking out the gardens, it was the only thing I could think to calm my growing anger.

"I did not come here to argue morality with you, Cailleach," he seethed, his breath hot against the nape of my neck. "Now," he said, leveling his tone. "Do you care to tell me what Arne deemed so important he called this urgent meeting?"

But my blood was already frozen with the sheer closeness of his existence. Eager to escape his presence, my fingers slipped against the rosebush I'd been nursing, the pad of my thumb catching sharply on one of the thorns. I let out a choked cry at the sudden sting of pain, a curse slipping from my lips.

I cradled my thumb in my hand, bending over the wound to inspect the damage. Crimson beaded against the punctured skin. I brought my injured thumb to my mouth, sucking on the wound and willing a bit of my magic into the appendage so it would heal.

Black, icy shadows crept toward me. I turned around slowly until my eyes met Death's as he towered over me. This close, his harsher features seemed less pronounced, less intimidating and... haunting. It was as if his mask had slipped, or some ward had been broken. I could perhaps—for a brief moment—see the being behind the deity. A complex expression invaded his usually composed features—something caught between intrigue and distress. For the first time, I could see life swirling in the deep onyx of his eyes.

As quickly as they had appeared, those distinguishing features were gone. The powerful mask of Death slipped back into place as he cleared his throat and took a step backwards.

"Quite clumsy, aren't you?" he jested. The corner of his lips turned up as his gaze swept over my body, landing finally at the wound that had already healed over on my thumb. "It's not very becoming for a goddess such as yourself. You should learn to take better care. Though, you've always been a bit brash, especially in your manner of speaking. Someone may indeed mistake you for a lesser being—for something like me."

The dark of his eyes flicked back to mine for a long, inescapable moment. Finally, his words registered and I stumbled backwards, scoffing in anger.

"Last I checked, being a goddess entitled me to act and speak however I damn well please. I wasn't aware I had to answer to you, or anyone else."

He didn't respond, just watched me as an irritating twinkle of amusement danced across his features. I rolled my eyes, turning my back to him and sending another curse over my shoulder as I walked back towards the palace, desperate to force space between us.

His wicked amusement might have been grating, but it was nothing compared to the strain I felt on my magic whenever he was near. I hastened my step, suppressing a shudder. I wrapped my arms around myself, pulling at the gossamer material of my gown in an attempt to cover my skin, suddenly unable to feel the comforting warmth of the midday sun on my bare arms.

CHAPTER 2
Death

Whether she believed me or not, I didn't come here just to antagonize Cailli. Arne, the god of power, had sent for me. Every few months or so, he insisted on meeting to discuss whatever trivial things he felt needed to be addressed, but this had been an unplanned, urgent request. He was a tad dramatic for my liking—all brawn, no brain, and constantly crying wolf where there was simply a rabbit. But alas, the food was always good and the scenery even better, so I didn't cause too much of a fuss about altering my schedule to make time for them. Plus, I didn't entirely mind watching Cailli flush at the sight of me.

I watched her skitter away, no doubt feeling the unsettling presence of my shadows dancing around her irresistible form. I couldn't pry my eyes away as her gown flowed around her body, the gossamer material winding around her as if one simple tug of the fabric would bring the whole thing fluttering to the ground. I knew my proximity bothered her the same as it did me, but for entirely different reasons. She was the only being in this world capable of pure creation, and I harbored nothing but death and decay. Even being near her made my magic feel unstable; the sheer power of life within her threatened the darkness inside me, causing it to swell, to consume.

Still, it wasn't that fact alone that made it impossible to be near her. It was the way she made me feel incomplete, as if there was something else, something deeper meant for me—for us. She was the forbidden fruit and I was the damned fool that would continue pining for it. I longed to touch her, taste her, in a way I was sure she'd never allow. And I hated myself for it.

Her bare feet padded through the grass, the soft sound soothing the buzz inside my ears. Her hips swayed with her haste, the gilded fabric of her dress shimmering in fractals of sunlight. The motion made my hand twitch, bringing my shadows to the surface as they wrapped around my fingers and became extensions of the appendages.

I grimaced, tamping down on that insatiable need to *claim*—trying my best to resist the scent of her blood still hanging in the air. It was a heady presence, earthy like the perfume of a rosebud buried deep within the dirt. I breathed in deeply, relishing in its potency as it invaded my nostrils, tormenting my soul.

I lingered in the garden a moment longer, forcing the power down as I watched her long, copper tresses sway in the soft breeze, brushing against her arms, her back. She disappeared beyond the palace doors a moment later and I released a long, slow breath—letting go of the power I'd held back in her presence. Darkness overtook the back half of the garden, leaving nothing but destruction as my shadows ravaged the robust shrubs and blooming flowers.

It was always like this when I was in her presence. My existence was desperate for her beauty, her power. I was far too consumed by the pain and loss of this world, so surrounded by it that being in the presence of pure creation was a sort of high to my system, a welcome relief to the utter misery that filled my days.

The Depths—my home—was not a desirable realm, full of the tormented wayward souls I'd spent my life claiming. And recently the mortal realm had become so chaotic and violent that I had no choice but to forge the Daeomi to help restore order and keep up with the death toll. They were a crude replica of what Cailli created in the other realms, formed out of the dust of the afterlife and the shadows of the Depths. They were dark, burdensome creatures—so much so that I often found myself debating wiping out the lot and starting over on my own.

But I didn't have such luxuries, forced to deal with the decay of the world these gods had created. Where the souls deemed unworthy by the other deities were sent to me, they kept the best of the mortal souls in their realm above—an elite few saved from damnation to serve and bend to the deities' every will.

I rarely glimpsed the pleasures even the elite enjoyed. Instead, these meetings were my only escape from the gruesome monotony of my life. There was little solace in the life of an immortal—even less for me, given the curse of my destructive power. In my centuries of rule, the only peace I'd found had come from leaning into my powers fully, in embracing my role as a claimer of souls, the merciless Grimm.

I rolled my shoulders, letting the power within me slip back into place. Once I was sure my shadows were done flexing and safely tucked away beneath my control, I made my way up towards the palace.

The doors, like always, were wide open as I strode into the marble-floored foyer. So much of this place was open at all times—to be more connected with the world beyond, they'd once claimed. I looked around to the draperies blowing in the slight breeze, the light from the day pouring into the palace halls in every direction, and saw nothing but opportunity for infiltration. They might claim they wanted to be close to the worlds beyond, in touch with life and nature, but they knew nothing of the cruelties of this world. They were ignorant children, sitting pretty in this grandiose palace full of wealth and power. They had no idea of the dark truths in the realms beyond, the violence and chaos that ensued daily. If the fae knew that they were so flippant in their security, they'd be invading without a second thought.

I walked those lands, I saw the vile corruption that they had to offer. The fae were power-hungry monsters who would only accept the crumbs of power Arne felt gracious enough to bestow on them for so long. I shook my head in silent criticism as I made my way down the familiar hall to our council chamber. I slowed as I approached the solid copper doors that led to the oversized table I knew was waiting on the other side. A small form lingered nearby, her back to me. I cleared my throat, announcing my presence as the figure jumped, spinning around hastily.

"I'm so sorry, Your Grace," she answered hurriedly as she righted herself and smoothed her hands over her dress. "Can I get you anything? Before the meeting starts?"

I gave a firm shake of my head, letting the mask of Death slip in place as she watched me a moment longer. I recognized her as Theora, one of the sister scribes. They were a lesser deity, scribes for the gods. The other deities thought nothing of them; they were simply background noise. I trusted them even less than I trusted the other deities, though. They recorded our every word, stored our every move in their archives. And it made me uneasy to think what they could do with that kind of power.

"Well then, I'll just finish my preparations before it starts. They are all there, waiting for you."

Before I could reply, she was rushing down the long hall, looking back at me over her shoulder. I kept my eyes on her, watching her with curious suspicion until she rounded a corner and was out of my view. I turned my attention back to the doors before me, running a hand over the intricate etchings in the cool metal. Hushed, unsteady whispers argued from the other side. "He's here." I recognized the Divine's voice, the rush in her words causing a brief smile to creep across my lips.

"It's about fucking time." Arne's booming voice echoed through the oversized room. I could feel it reverberate against the door beneath my hand, causing me to shake my head. No finesse with that one. "We have shit to do and this is his responsibility as well as ours. I'm sick of waiting for the so-called Ruler of the Underworld to grace us with his presence whenever he sees fit."

I pushed through the doors, gliding into the chamber with silky ease. "Did someone call for me?" I mused, slipping my hands into the pockets of my pants as I felt the obsidian mist snake across the pristine marble floor.

Arne sat at the head of the table, accompanied by the other deities—Lukus, the god of war and mischief; Estrid, the goddess of love and fertility; and Cailleach, the Divine, all perched in their respective thrones with their noses high in the air, reeking of regal stench. That is, until their eyes fell to me. This was what I loved, watching the looks of fear creep over their features as my power pulsed through the room, snaking around their thrones and tugging on their life force.

They wanted a monster? I'd give them a monster. I let my power radiate a moment longer, taking my time to find my seat at their table.

I sank into the chair, making it evidently clear just how comfortable I was able to make myself in their home, how easy it was for me to fit in here amongst them—if I wanted to. For extra measure, I helped myself to the pot of tea waiting on the table. I smacked my lips together as I drank, savoring the tart flavor of the fruity tea—even though I despised its flavor.

"Now," I called out over the room as I set my cup down, breaking the spell that held them captive. "What was so important that you required my immediate presence?" I picked a grape off a tray of assorted fruit, popping it in my mouth and crushing it between my molars as I made eye contact with Arne, gesturing for him to get on with it.

Arne cleared his throat, fiddling with the parchments laid out across the table in front of him. "Yes, well, had you been here on time you would have heard me discuss the issue at hand." He thumbed through a stack of parchment, finding the paper he was looking for and tossing it down the table so it landed in front of me. I let out a deep sigh as I sat up, grabbed it, and skimmed its contents.

Looking back to Arne over the page, I fought the urge to roll my eyes. "Death tolls? That's what you needed me here for?"

"As trivial as it may seem to you, Death, these numbers are rising exponentially—"

"I don't need some silly parchment to tell me that death is on the rise amongst the realms." I leaned forward, tossing the parchment back at Arne. I sneered as he watched the records flitter across the table. "Or have you forgotten whose duty it is to claim those souls?"

"Then why did you not tell us sooner?" Estrid asked, her brows furrowed.

"Exactly," replied Lukus, leveling a glare at me. "You know how the realm would be threatened by a fae revolt!"

I sat back in my chair, crossing my legs and resting my clasped hands against my knee as I scoffed.

It must be so nice to have the privilege of this realm, a buffer from the chaos and violence that ensued every moment beyond that border. They ruled over the realms, bestowed power to these beings, and then they sat up here in their ivory towers—concealed by their lies and deception.

"You all have never cared to listen to my reports on the raw carnage of the world beyond."

"Is that true?" Estrid echoed nervously, looking between Arne and Lukus. "Have we heard such reports before?"

"He's lying," mumbled Lukus unconvincingly, surely remembering the way they brushed off my concerns many decades past. "Who's to say *he's* not the one instigating this surge in numbers?"

"I have tried to warn you of the state of the fae for *years* now," I ground out bitterly. "But my pleas for intervention have long been ignored. And now you wish to claim I am the irresponsible party?"

Anger seethed from me, mirrored in the shadows darkening the room.

Arne rose in challenge. "Death, I swear, lower your shadows, or—"

"You lot choose to hide up here"—my voice rose, cutting off Arne—"fucking and drinking your way through eternity rather than fulfilling your duties over their realms. The raw carnage of the world beyond, that has everything to do with your negligence." I let my shadows remain a moment longer, looking to each of them and sending the pile of untouched parchment back in their faces with a wave of my power. "You created this mess, yet I'm the one left to clean it up."

"Don't play like you suddenly have a soft heart for the lesser beings," Arne spat back. My blood boiled beneath my skin, my mind battling between revealing too much or keeping my mask in place. "The difference between us and you is that you're not the one being threatened by their power when the fae revolt. They'll come after us, here. Meanwhile you get to slink away to the Depths and leave the rest of us to take responsibility for your actions. You delight in their chaos, Death. Don't pretend otherwise."

I let their accusations hang in the air, lowering my gaze and shaking my head as I let a low chuckle slip between my lips. There was so much irony in their accusations, their fear.

"Lukus, are you not the one in control of their war efforts?" I spoke at last, raising my head to level my gaze on the trickster bastard, my lips tipping up at the challenge rolling off my tongue. "Arne, their power? If the issue is that the fae are rising to take you down, why not just use that almighty power of yours to strike them down before they even have the chance? You are a god after all, aren't you?"

Arne's face twisted up in anger—his skin going red-hot, his hands glowing with the power always within reach as he opened his mouth to fight back.

"That's enough." Cailli's soft voice was surprisingly powerful as it rang out around us. The melodic sound shook me from my building anger, reminding me to keep my facade in place. For her sake.

I wanted nothing more than to lunge across the table and tell her everything I feared, but I knew it would be no use. Broaching the subject in her presence was impossible, some piece of invisible magic twining inside me like poison if I even thought about trying to reveal it all to her. I feared the gods had somehow cursed us from speaking on such things. But even if she could hear my words, I wasn't sure she'd believe them while she was still under their thumb, her power so weakened. It would take finding my proof, piecing it together fully for her and helping her find her power, to stand any chance of changing things.

We fell silent as we all tried to rein in our power. Slowly, she pressed her palms against the table and rose to her feet. "There is enough discord going on right now without us turning on each other. We need to come together to deal with this, not rip each other apart."

I inhaled deeply, slowly, my nostrils flaring as I watched the rest of the deities settle back into their seats. My eyes landed on one of the sisters taking notes in the corner, the one I'd found eavesdropping outside the door. I hadn't realized she'd been here to witness the discord between us. I bristled, frustrated I'd been too foolishly distracted to notice her presence. I didn't want my temper taken down in their records, didn't need any permanent detail of my opposition to the other deities.

Cailli was right, we needed to work together. But not because it was for the best of the realms. It was because I couldn't give them any reason to grow suspicious.

"Then tell us from the start, Death," said Arne, his voice adopting an unusually calm tone. "Before the realms fall into destruction even we cannot fix."

The doors to the council chamber flew open beneath the power of my shadows, clearing the way for me as I sauntered out of the room and left the asshole deities behind me. Hours of bickering and power plays had gotten us absolutely nowhere and I'd reached my limit of tolerance for their games.

The death and destruction that ravaged the mortal realms had grown tenfold in the last few decades, as I'd made more than clear time after time. Their refusal to acknowledge this issue was what had spurred me down the path I was on now. I'd gone digging for information on what I could do to reason with them, appease their power so they'd actually do something to help the mortal realms. The surprising lack of information I'd found on the deities shouldn't have come as a surprise, nor should their deceit. I'd learned long ago to not care for a single living being. Cailli was the exception, not the rule. If my life as the Ruler of the Underworld had taught me anything, it was that you could trust no one. And care for even less.

And in their eyes, I served as their monster, their scapegoat. It worked to keep the distance between me and the Divine, which would always be their ultimate goal. But it was their negligence, their lack of control over the realms that had resulted in this level of chaos. The call for my presence amongst the mortal realms was a repercussion of the deities actions—or lack thereof. Yet no matter how much I argued that point, no matter what I said or did to prove the dutiful use of my power, the others refused to listen. They would always see me as a villain. It was in the very essence of my nature to exist in bloodshed—to clean up the mess the others created because they only viewed the lessers as pawns to be played with. Despite how much I despised this role.

It was time for me to return to the realms in which I belonged—time to return to the role that I played in all of this. Even as my footsteps pounded against the dirt, mimicking the rhythm of my beating heart, I could hear the call. It echoed through my body, bringing forth the dark need to respond as I made my way towards the border of this realm. My magic twitched in response, a reaction impossible to deny. Chaos and discord ruled beyond this place and there was only one entity that could tamp down on that power and put these creatures back in their rightful place.

I shifted my gait as I stepped through the realms, letting my magic bend and stretch to allow the true face of Death to surface. I paused, breathing in the bitter scent of carnage before rolling my shoulders and locking my jaw. I let my magic take over as it led me to the first of many souls that would be claimed tonight.

CHAPTER 3
The Divine

I cradled my head in my hands as I leaned over the massive oak table in the council chamber. The others had long since left, our meeting ending in more bickering than solutions. Nothing had been resolved, or even truly discussed. Arne was more focused on pointing blame than dealing with the issues at hand. I'd once thought perhaps Estrid would be my ally in all of this, but these days she seemed more consumed with the approval of Lukus and Arne than actually holding an opinion for herself. And Death... I wasn't sure what to believe when it came to him.

His presence alone sent shivers down my spine, making me believe him capable of such carnage. Arne had always been steadfast in his accusations against Death, filling the rest of us in on the vile, vicious things he did to the souls within the Depths. But Death had been convincing in his defense of himself, insistent that he did only what his duties called for. He claimed the souls allotted to him, those in the mortal realm that were deserving of an eternity in the Depths. And that the source of the fae uprising was nothing more than the consequence of our lack of intervention amongst the mortal realms.

I didn't know what to believe. At one point in our existence we had been more hands-on. If I thought back far enough, I could remember a time when I walked the mortal realms, relishing in my creation's worship. It was wonderful, peaceful. But those memories were from so long ago, too fuzzy to remember fully. All I knew was something changed, and Arne advised we stay within the Realm of the Gods, to be overseers of the realms. It was safer this way, to let creation live on without our overbearing presence, to let them live as they saw fit and to protect us from their growing numbers. It had made sense at the time, but perhaps that era was coming to a close.

I raised my head, letting my eyes fall to the records strewn across the table. Parchment upon parchment full of the devastating losses that ravaged the other realms. The others didn't understand the blow it was to see the full weight of that destruction. Yes, perhaps they'd gifted things to the other realms. They all had their own duties, their own responsibilities and gifts to bestow upon the creatures of our world. But they were my creatures, my creation. No one else's. And their loss weighed heavy on me in a way I knew none of the others would ever be able to feel.

A singular hot tear rolled down my cheek as I forced myself to read over the death toll again, letting each and every name burn into my heart as I tried to fathom the countless lives that had been lost. For too long I had turned a blind eye, too consumed by the realm around me. It was true, Death had tried to warn us. I'd overheard his hushed and frantic conversations with Arne and Lukus on more than one occasion. When I'd inquired about them, about the accusations Death had made against *my* creation, they'd assured me it was false. That there was nothing to worry about and these accusations were nothing more than a desperate attempt from an unhappy god to find a place amongst us. To feel important and to cause strife.

But now, seeing scroll after scroll of the repercussions of my own negligence. It was consuming, filling me with a deep-seated grief and regret I didn't think I'd ever shake.

A small noise pulled me from the parchment as I spun around to find Lukus standing in the doorway. "Cailleach." He cleared his throat. "Please excuse me, I didn't mean to frighten you."

I gestured for him to enter. "Oh, not at all. I lingered behind to go over the records for today." He stalked through the room, looking out the oversized windows on the far side of the large table, hands clasped behind his back. I observed him for a moment, eyes wary as I marked his movements. Strands of his long blonde hair billowed in the soft breeze as he surveyed the land below before turning back towards me. It was off-putting, his presence here, and I was grateful for one of the sisters' entrance to deliver tea a moment later.

Karmi stopped short, looking awkwardly between me and Lukus, before setting a small tray down on the table beside me. Lukus came up beside the table as she poured a cup of the dark tea. The blend was one of my favorites, so much deeper and earthier than the bright, tart blend the other deities preferred.

"I'm sorry, Your Grace. I didn't know you were to be joining the Divine. I'll fetch another teacup at once." She set the teapot down and scurried out of the room as Lukus took the seat beside me. He picked up my steaming cup of tea, taking a deep sip. I resisted the urge to roll my eyes at his entitlement. It was, unfortunately, something I'd grown accustomed to over our time together.

"I never fully understood the purpose of the sisters," he said when he'd finally pulled the cup away from his lips. "But damn, do they make a good cup of tea."

I pursed my lips, feigning a smile as he set the cup down, filling the room with the sound of clinking glass. "Is there something I can do for you, Lukus?" My patience was wearing thin at his sudden interest in me.

"The death toll," he answered simply. I huffed out a breath, frustrated after the excruciating monotony that had been our meeting earlier. He'd voiced his concerns well enough; I didn't understand why he felt the need to return and bother me with more of his bickering. "I cannot say I know what is causing this uptick in violence. Such was made quite clear earlier today. And normally I'd advise you not to concern yourself with these affairs. But..." His words dropped off, his finger tracing idle circles on the rim of his teacup before he leaned in abruptly, lowering his voice: "These are your creatures, are they not? You, more than anyone, understand what makes them tick."

"What is your point?" I asked through gritted teeth.

"I would venture to ask you..." He paused, raising those beady eyes to meet mine. Something hidden and envious stared back at me, something I couldn't quite place. "When was the last time you visited the other realms, the last time you saw for yourself their struggles? Or the last time they saw your presence in their lives, for that matter?"

His question caught me off guard. I couldn't respond, I had no answer. I hadn't walked amongst them in what felt like an eternity. I'd come to believe it was forbidden, something none of the deities would dare to consider after Arne's warnings. We wanted to allow them space to live, to thrive, without fear of us or our abilities. We were watching over them from the cosmos—or maybe that was the lie we'd told ourselves when we'd shut ourselves away in this higher realm.

Perhaps it had been far too long. Perhaps this uprising was of our own doing—my own—just as Death had claimed. If that was true, then maybe returning to them, walking amongst them, was the solution that we needed. It was certainly one that none of us had considered. Death was the only god who walked amongst them—and it wasn't like his presence in the mortal realm was necessarily desired.

Karmi's voice cut across the room, startling me. "Here you are, Your Grace." Her voice was eager, if not slightly out of breath, as she set a new teacup down in front of us alongside a fresh pot of tea. My jaw clenched in irritation as a bright pink stream flowed from the spout of the teapot and filled the cup, the aroma of the fruity blend wafting between us. Her brow furrowed for a second as she moved to hand it to Lukus, realizing too late that he already had a cup in his hand.

I reached out, taking the cup from her hand and offering her a small smile. "Thank you, Karmi." She returned it with her own faint smile as she bowed, retreating to the far end of the room to clean up dishes from the meeting earlier.

"All I'm saying is that if it were me…" Lukus's low voice pulled my attention back to our conversation. His eyes raked over Karmi's presence in a way that had my own skin crawling. I cleared my throat before taking a sip from the tea she'd prepared for me. My stomach instantly roiled at the taste, my irritation spiking at his audacity for claiming the teapot that I would have preferred. Lukus had always believed he could own anything he wanted. Whether it be my tea or the sister on the far end of the room, his entitlement knew no bounds. And for that reason, my awareness stood at full attention any time he was around.

Lukus's eyes slowly made their way back to mine. A crooked grin teased his lips as I raised an eyebrow at him. "I'd want to see it for myself. It's hard to solve a problem you haven't even set your eyes upon. Perhaps that's the first step to all of this." He raised his cup to me, taking one last long sip before pushing himself out of the seat and slinking down the hall.

I let my gaze linger where he'd disappeared from my sight, suddenly struck with the truth. It didn't matter who had delivered it, or how ill-mannered the delivery had been. He was right. I was meant to be a ruler, a goddess—the one with the solutions and the one making the hard calls. Yet here I was, stashed away in a different realm and completely out of touch with what my creation was experiencing.

My eyes fell once more to the papers strewn across the table. I sat there, mulling over his words and reading name after name over and over again until I drained my teacup. "Karmi," I called, finally lifting my head from the table. She'd busied herself with idle work on the far side of the chamber, waiting for me to finish.

"Yes, Your Grace?" she answered as she made her way over to where I sat. I patted the chair beside me, inviting her to join me at the table. She hesitated, throwing a long look over her shoulder in the direction Lukus had gone. Seats at this table were meant for the council only, for the deities reigning in power. I rolled my eyes, pushing the chair out for her. "Let's not get caught up in silly customs and procedures."

She eyed me warily.

"I won't tell anyone if you won't," I added, throwing a quick wink her way. Her face softened at that, a hint of a smile cracking across her face as she took a quick look around the room and out the door before hurriedly taking her seat.

I couldn't remember when I'd stopped asking the sisters for their advice on matters. They used to be the first I'd go to—being scribes to the gods—but over time I concerned myself with the issues of the realms less and less.

It had never occurred to me till now that they must have spent all this time recording and learning, growing even wiser while I lost my grip on the realms.

"I wanted to ask you something about these," I explained as I held up the parchment.

She blinked as she looked between the records and me. "You want *my* help?" she asked in utter shock.

I suppressed the urge to chuckle, nodding. "Yes, Karmi. This is your forte, is it not? Recordkeeper? I thought perhaps you'd have some insight into this increase in violence. Or at the very least some idea of how we might combat it."

I sighed as I laid the parchments in front of her. She took them gingerly between her fingers, never taking her eyes off me. "Go ahead, read them," I insisted.

"I don't need to, Cailleach," she offered humbly. "These records are seared into the minds of me and my sisters." I sat up a little straighter, finding myself slightly shocked and impressed by the measure of their magic. "We are the ones responsible for keeping them, the parchment is just a formality," she added as she set them back on the table. "For you." She pushed the records back towards me as I let my gaze fall to the intricate writing dancing across the pages.

"I apologize for not being more educated on the inner workings of your duties, Karmi, of your magic," I said after several moments of silence. It took me time to find my voice, to admit how utterly unprepared I still felt in this role. Perhaps it was something I'd known at one time, the small details of this world slipping away after so many centuries of reigning. Perhaps it was something I'd never taken the time to worry myself with. No matter the reason, I scolded myself for appearing so unprepared and uneducated in front of the beings in my charge.

"Forgive me, Karmi." I let my head fall to my hand as I leaned against the table. "No matter how long I've been doing this, I fear there is always something I'm missing, details lost in time."

Warmth spread up my arm as I realized she had laid her hand atop mine. "It's alright, Your Grace." Her kind eyes met mine as I offered her a friendly smile.

"You know, being a higher deity doesn't leave much room for things like friendship." I looked back down the hallway. "It may seem like nothing but wondrous power and endless opportunity but..." I trailed off, wondering suddenly why I felt secure enough to admit this to her. I wanted to tamp down on the confession, let it die on my tongue as I searched desperately for my composure. But it was like trying to clean up spilled oil. It was slick and messy and impossible to reclaim once it had started to pour out. "But it's such a lonely existence," I said at last, swallowing hard against the knot in my throat.

Karmi watched me behind sympathetic eyes, clearly uncertain what to say to such a sudden confession. "I consider myself lucky to have the companionship of my sisters. My family is oftentimes the only thing that keeps me going," she finally admitted.

She paused before continuing, as if she was trying to determine how freely to let herself talk. "It's just..." She shifted in her chair before leaning forward and squeezing my hand as she continued in a hushed tone, "Forgive me if I overstep, but the deities don't seem to consider each other family as my sisters and I do. I can only imagine, Your Grace, how lonely that must feel."

Her words struck a chord within me, freezing my blood as I stared off with wide eyes and a deep hurt burrowing somewhere within me. I hadn't even noticed when she'd released her grip on my hand, when she'd stood and made her way over to the tray of dirty dishes and carried them to the doorway.

She turned back to me for a moment longer, the tray balanced on her hip. "Be careful, Cailleach. I don't know how to slow the chaos amongst the mortal realms, but I know there's unrest stirring here, as well." Her eyes wandered over the walls, up the ceiling, and down the hallway. "I don't know how to describe it, but I can feel it in my bones."

She tapped quietly against the silver tray, lost in thought for a moment. As if she was replaying her words in her mind to verify their truth. She nodded a moment later, dipping in a small bow, and took her leave. Her footsteps echoed down the corridor for a long moment, their steady rhythm an eerie melody for the warning she left behind.

I let her advice ruminate in my mind as I sat in silence and watched the sunset beyond the open windows of the palace. The only presence in the room with me was the soft, sweet breeze blowing through the gossamer curtains. Finally, I stood with a steadfast determination. Abandoning the scrolls of ink and parchment, I turned away from the safety of the council chamber. My footsteps were quiet but steady as I made my way through the palace and out into the twilight of the evening.

If I didn't do this now, I'd talk myself out of it altogether. I'd spent entirely too long hidden away amongst the cosmos. It was time for me to return to the realm of my creation. They were my responsibility, mine to look after and take care of. And they had fallen into a never-ending spiral of devastation and loss. I wouldn't sit idly by while scroll after scroll of death tolls and reports of destruction passed through my fingers. It wasn't enough to memorize their names, wasn't enough to mourn their loss. It was time for me to see it for myself.

CHAPTER 4
The Divine

I slipped into the nearby forest, hoping the trees would provide ample cover as I attempted to open the border between the realms. I closed my eyes, concentrating on the magic that separated our worlds. My hands were clammy as I balled my fingers into fists, trying to muster up the courage I'd had only moments ago. I could feel the magic of the wards pulse before me, uneasy with my presence here. Their purpose was to keep out any lesser beings, but it had been too long since one of us stepped through its portal.

I slowed my breathing, closing my eyes and forcing my heart to calm as I stepped through. Slipping between time and space itself, my body screamed at its physical restraints, until my magic took over and soothed the ache clawing its way through my body. Realities swirled around me as I let the magic carry me to the mortal realm. With one more step forward, my feet landed against rough earth and the magic around me stilled. The pain faded away as the world around me came into focus.

I blinked slowly as I took in my surroundings. I'd done it, I had walked between realms and stood on the land of the mortals for the first time in more decades than I cared to admit. This was the first step in a long line of restoration that I would bring to my people.

Lukus had been right, *this* was right. Only…it looks so hauntingly different from what I'd remembered.

My smile fell, the excitement melting away as the reality around me sunk in.

It was taking everything within me to not turn back and run to the safety of our realm, the inviting warmth of our palace with the only beings I'd ever known. I might not exactly consider them family, but they were better company than the ice cold hatred I felt in this world.

I didn't need to see its people to feel it. I could sense it in the air, threading itself through the roots tangled in the earth beneath my feet. Corruption and hatred had consumed this realm, permeating the very essence of its being. My magic blossomed in answer, my hands glowing with power as I reached out to bring life to the depraved world around me.

My magic twined with the poisoned land, trying to bring forth life in place of its darkness. But my magic died out, fading into the cracked ground with an overwhelming sense of defeat. The land was too far gone, too deteriorated and cursed to respond to even my magic.

My heart cracked with each step I took, shattering into a million pieces as I saw every detail of this reality, of the true extent of my defeat even now as I continued to try and repair it. This isn't what I'd wanted for this world, this hadn't been my intention when I'd let my power flow and breathed life into this realm.

I'd been naive enough to step away, convinced they'd be more comfortable without my power looming over them. The weight of this responsibility nearly crushed me. Everywhere I looked, I saw reminders of my utter failure.

I moved forward through the wilderness around me, each step taking me further into the destruction of my entire life's work. The air hung heavy with decay, the acrid scent of smoke and blood stinging my nose. The forest around me had become nothing more than charred, petrified wood, splitting out of the earth below like spikes left to warn intruders away. Past the thicket of trees, I could make out the angry orange hue of fire. Whether it was for protection or destruction, I couldn't tell. But the flames danced in a cascade of power as I followed their light through the trees.

Tears slipped down my cheeks as I took in this dark and desolate world, so different from the wonder and beauty I'd left it as. Why hadn't I been here? I didn't even know how I would have protected it—preserved it—when my magic had no power but to create more life, but I couldn't help but blame myself for its utter destruction.

Up ahead the source of the fire came into view. A stone wall stretched in either direction, illuminated by rows of burning torches. I stepped closer, running my fingers over the rough stone. It was clearly some kind of fortress. Curiosity overtook me as I followed the length of it, hoping I might find some sort of entrance if I followed the wall further.

I peeked around an opening in the wall and glimpsed a destitute village within. Rows of dilapidated homes sat dark and cold. The putrid smell intensified as I tiptoed forward, keeping close to the stone wall to stay out of sight. No light or laughter could be found in what lay beyond. Only the cries of hopelessness and the silence of misery met me.

I squinted my eyes, the smell stinging them and causing my vision to blur with tears, and moved carefully from one building to another. The outskirts of this village were surrounded by ramshackle dwellings, full of dirtied, sick, and starving bodies. They peered out at me, their eyes hardened and hateful, but no one spoke, only watching me cautiously as I wandered deeper into the village. Up ahead, I could make out the massive estate of whatever fae ruled here. I gasped as my eyes pored over the stone stairs, noticing for the first time the cages lining the entrance—the source of the moans and cries filling the air.

Mortals. I knew because I could sense no magic from them. Helpless mortals being held for torment and fae entertainment. Some banged against the bars, full of fight and fury at being held in such conditions. Others were slumped over, barely able to do more than moan in pain and misery. I pulled my eyes away from the ones who didn't move at all, their dead and decaying bodies hanging through the metal or pierced on pikes along the stairs.

Guards and what looked to be higher fae circled some of the cages off to the left, admiring their work. A piercing scream cut through the air as one younger mortal man was pulled from his cage by a few guards and forced inside the fortress. His screams echoed through the village as he begged and pleaded to be released, to return home to his family. They fell on deaf ears as they pushed him through the double doors, a set of fae females trailing close behind and passing a handful of gold coins to one of the guards.

My stomach turned, my body instinctively retreating away from the depraved village. My feet smacked in a loud, wet rhythm against the thick mud as I turned and ran back to the break in the stone wall. I had no business coming here, no business being amongst this realm, amongst this abhorrent kingdom. I had severely underestimated the current state of things and I was quickly realizing how stupid I'd been for coming here so unprepared.

My eyes searched frantically for the exit, an involuntary squeal of relief escaping me when I finally found my way back out. I threw myself against the outside of the stone wall, pressing my body against its comforting stability as I tried to catch my breath.

I wondered if the other deities truly knew how bad things were here. They'd spoken on how vicious the fae had become, how high the death tolls were getting. I wracked my mind, overturning every piece of information they had shared about this realm, but nothing they'd said could have prepared me for this. Mortals being taken from their own realms, being held captive for such sinister entertainment. Fae of lesser magic and means being forced to live in poverty and rot rather than being cared for by their rulers.

I had to get back to the Realm of the Gods, had to tell the other deities of the atrocities I'd found here. I knew they wouldn't listen to me. Centuries of living beside them told me they wouldn't. But I'd make them listen. I'd find a way to get through to them, to make my input matter.

Two fae guards stumbled through the opening in the fortress wall beside me. They reeked of sweat and drink, something vile swimming in their eyes as they noticed my presence.

I retreated a few steps, my body screaming at me to run. But my feet were rooted to the spot, an icy fear taking over my ability to move.

"Well, well, well," the one on the right boasted. His breath was hot and rancid as it hit my face. "What do we have here, Rotian?" He stepped forward, circling me as I spun to keep his body in front of mine. "It appears that we've stumbled upon a bit of luck."

His friend sniggered beside me and I whipped my head back towards him. "I mean no trouble," I promised, as I raised my hands in front of me. "I've come from the Realm of the Gods, but I assure you I will not harm you."

"The Realm of the Gods?" the fae in front of me scoffed. "What gods?" He threw his hands out. "There are no gods left amongst the realms, miss. They have long since abandoned us. Or haven't you noticed?" His voice rang out, bouncing off the stone wall behind me and piercing the night air. "And as for harming us... well, darling, I can promise it's not us you should be worried about."

My eyes went wide with his accusation. I took a step back, the rough stone cutting into my back, my palms. They pinned me to the wall, closing in. True terror pierced my core. My blood ran cold as I saw the intent in the eyes of the fae in front of me. My magic sparked to life within me, its golden light filling my veins with its useless power—a defensive reflex that would do nothing for me in this moment.

I turned to the left intent on running, desperate to get away from the vile creatures before me, just as something powerful collided with me. Whatever it was threw me back against the stone wall.

A blinding heat ignited at the back of my head, followed by a wet sensation as the scent of iron stung my nose. I tried to run again, stumbling as I forced my vision to focus, but only managed to trip over my own feet as I fell to the rocky mud below.

The two fae bent over me, the sight of them floating and fuzzy as I tried to scramble away from their grasp. The one called Rotian chuckled again before grabbing a handful of my hair and dragging me towards the trees. I cried out, from fear or pain I wasn't sure. My legs scraped against the earth, my dress catching and ripping on shriveled-up roots and fallen logs. I felt the unforgiving ground cutting into my bare skin as they continued to drag me further into the cover of the forest.

"Please," I begged as they threw me against a nearby trunk. "I'm sorry, I didn't know," I swore. They were angry. Rightfully so. I'd all but abandoned them here. I'd left them to this destruction when I should have been here to care for them. I choked on sobs as I tried to explain.

"Cry all you want, darling—scream for all we care. No one is going to come save you." The unnamed fae reached his hand out, willing some nearby vines to slither toward me. Despite my frantic attempts to escape their clutches, they found my wrists, my waist, coiling around my body and holding me in place as Rotain began removing his armor and unfastened his pants.

"No, please, just tell me what you want from me. I can help. I can fix this!" I cried out as the other fae's hand struck my face. The motion caused my lip to split, blood springing from the wound and filling my mouth with a tangy taste that had my stomach heaving. I'd made a mistake coming here. I was naive to believe I could come unarmed and unprepared, just as I had been naive to believe I'd ever be able to do anything to help restore balance to this realm. I was a goddess, a deity responsible for the creation of this world. Yet, in this moment, I'd never felt so powerless.

Tears streamed down my face as the fae switched places and Rotain stood before me. Evil glared in his eyes as he bent over me. A blade shone in his hand as he brought it up and swiped it down my front, tearing the remainder of my dress and exposing my dirtied flesh to them. He didn't speak as he took in the sight of me, but the feel of his eyes on my skin said more than enough. His gaze burrowed and burned and I squirmed against the rotting vines cutting into my skin, squeezing my eyes shut in some pitiful effort to escape the image before me.

The rough feel of the dead plants fell away as I fought against them and when I opened my eyes again, the two fae looked down with gaping expressions at where the restraints clung to me. In place of the decaying roots was flourishing greenery, still pinning me to their will, but no longer cursed with death.

"The Divine?" the nameless one whispered. There was a flash of uncertainty in his tone, and for a moment, the fear subsided. They finally understood who I was, maybe even why I'd come to their realm. I swallowed against the lump in my throat, letting out a breath of relief as recognition dawned on them. But Rotian's face turned even darker as his understanding gave way for corrupt desire.

He stepped forward, his determination doubled down as he now understood the gravity of the situation at hand—a fae with a goddess caught beneath his grasp, forced to fulfill his every whim. I fought harder against the vines as he willed his magic to tighten their hold. Plant matter cut into my skin, barbs and spurs burrowing into my wrists as I tried to break free. Only more joined them, pulling my kicking feet down to the earth and binding them there. Every shred of dignity fell away as I screamed out in utter desperation. I summoned as much strength and power as I could to fight back, but aside from breathing life back into my restraints, my power was useless here.

Rotian's weight shifted over me and the feel of his grimy body on mine threatened to expel the contents of my stomach. An uncontrollable tremble ravaged my body as the remaining fragment of my strength gave way to frigid fear. I let my head fall back and squeezed my eyes shut once more as I prepared for this darkness to consume me.

But it never came. Rotian's presence froze above me. I opened my eyes to find the same kind of fear I felt echoed in the fae's eyes as the air chilled with a new kind of power, a somehow familiar one.

I couldn't see past them into the trees to see what had changed or who was there. But I didn't need to.

I would recognize the feel of Death's power anywhere.

CHAPTER 5
Death

"Now, boys, is that any way to treat a goddess?" I let the threatening intent of my tone slip through the trees as I breathed in the delicious scent of their fear. My shadows snaked around the filthy fae cowards, toying with them like a cat playing with a mouse. Every push, every lick had their panic growing.

And I ate that shit up.

I didn't usually play with my victims. Most days I was more focused on doing my job quietly so I could return to the duties of my realm. I enjoyed a change of scenery from the Depths, but interacting with the beings that resided here was a particularly grating aspect of my life. The Daeomi might be annoying bastards, but they were predictable and knew to leave me alone most of the time. The mortals and the fae and the other creatures that roamed this realm were irksome, and I preferred to stay separated from them as much as possible.

That is, unless they did something to provoke me.

My tolerance was nonexistent when they overstepped their place. And right now, seeing the Divine pinned beneath their hold was threatening any semblance of control I had over that darkness inside me.

I stepped forward, letting the darkness give way, growing around me and seeping into the trees, the ground, the very air they breathed. My steps were slow, stormless, as I closed the distance between us. Complete and total silence fell over the clearing as I used my power to turn the fae away from Cailli, cloaking her in a blanket of shadow to shield her pristine skin from the elements and their hungry eyes.

The fae took in the full face of Death as I stepped up to them. I forced my composure to remain, the unbothered mask of a ruthless god dealing with nothing more than aggravating vermin. I wouldn't let them see how deep that fury ran, not yet.

"Explain," I commanded as I raised my hand, releasing the power holding their tongues. A chorus of shrill pleas and half assed excuses broke across the clearing and I instantly clenched the air, willing my power to slip around their lungs. "One at a time," I grated out through clenched teeth. I turned towards the one on the left, pointing with the hand that wasn't currently crushing their chests.

I waited for his explanation, staring into the bottomless pit of despair in his eyes. His mouth opened and closed, trying to find the words that weren't there. "I—"

His voice was cut off by a sputtering sound as my fist burst through his chest. My fingers sunk into his ribcage, wrapping around the still beating heart and tightening to the feel of that beautiful rhythm.

"I fear I may have misled you boys," I whispered as I leaned in between them. "You see, no explanation would have excused your behavior today. No lies you would have spun would save you from my wrath." I leaned back, jerking my hand out of the fae's body—his heart still clenched in my fist. I raised it between us as the beating slowed, my shadows overtaking it and turning it to dust beneath my fingers. The eyes of the fae went wide as he looked down to the now gaping hole in his body. His friend's gaze followed, his frenzied screams piercing the air the same moment the body hit the ground.

I sidestepped the twitching fae remains, blood pooling over the rocky earth. His friend shouted and cursed behind me, but I ignored the irritating buzz of his words as I let a shadow snake around his throat and gag his mouth. My power forced him to his knees; I could barely contain a smile as I heard the squelch of him landing in the gore of his friend's consequences.

"You—killed him?"

I turned, almost forgetting her presence for a moment. Cailli was balled up in the same spot. Tears and dirt streaked her face, her usual golden glow replaced with a pale, haunting white as she took in the scene before her. Her shaky words mirrored her shock as she looked from the crumpled remains of the slain fae, barely formed enough to still be called a body, and the blood still dripping from my fingers. She started shaking her head, curling tighter into herself. I paused, suddenly realizing how utterly stupid I'd been to subject her to more horror. She'd already been through enough tonight, and I loathed my blindness to that sensitivity. I let out a deep breath through my nose, before cocking my head back over my shoulder and letting out a sharp whistle.

Within an instant, one of my Daeomi appeared along with a Depthhound. "Clean up this mess," I threw over my shoulder, not taking my eyes off Cailli. "And take that one with you." I pointed at the one who had touched her, the one I'd dragged off of her just in time to spare her from the vile thing he'd been hoping to subject her to. I planned to make him suffer for the moments of torment he put her through—and the moments he'd wished he'd inflicted still.

He wouldn't get as simple a death as his friend.

"No one touches him till I return," I added, lacing my words with enough threatening intent to let the Daeomi know what would happen if I was disobeyed. I had big plans for that one and I'd be damned if any of those bloodthirsty beasts ruined that for me.

The Daeomi got to work without another word as the fae that still remained let a new string of cries and curses ripple through the night. I pulled a piece of cloth from my breast pocket and wiped away the blood coating my hand and forearm, tucking the cloth back in its home as I knelt before Cailli. "I know this is impossible to ask of you right now, but we need to get moving. I'd rather not deal with more of their kind tonight."

Cailli looked up at me through a hollow gaze, my words not quite registering in her mind. I suppressed the urge to roll my eyes, my irritation reaching new heights at her stupidity in coming here without any kind of protection or idea of what she was getting herself into. I turned, giving myself a moment to collect myself as I scrubbed a hand over my face. The air was stale tonight, the wind practically nonexistent as I watched the trees just beyond the Daeomi. Movement somewhere beyond them had caught my attention and I was suddenly overwhelmed with the notion that perhaps we were not alone afterall. I let my senses stretch out, forcing the shadows to whisper to me. Whoever was out there was not fae, that much I could tell. But they were somehow evading my reach, and it had my skin itching to be free of this realm.

I turned back to Cailli, extending my hand. "You might not like it, but I'm your best option right now, goddess. Are you going to take it or shall I be on my way and leave you to whatever vicious fae comes across you next?"

She shook her head hurriedly as she reached for my hand. I pulled her to her feet, my shadows still cloaking her in darkness.

"Where are we going?" she asked through hooded eyes.

A toothy grin broke across my face as I pictured the Divine entering the gates of the Depths. "Let me ask you a question, goddess." I turned to face her, taking her hand delicately in my own once more. "Have you ever experienced true darkness?"

CHAPTER 6
Karmi

The air was heavy with darkness as my hands skimmed over rough, damp stone. I was feeling my way along the walls of the lower levels of the palace, searching for the meeting spot my sisters had insisted on. I hated this secrecy, hated feeling like at any moment we might be caught and punished for our treasonous acts. Taking a deep breath, I slowly turned another corner, squinting to allow my eyes to adjust to the even darker surroundings as I worked my way into the depths of the palace. It would all be worth it, I told myself as I exhaled. The lies, the scheming, the *risks*. Everything would pay off once my sisters and I had accomplished our goal.

The Divine was gone, taken to the Depths by Death himself. I didn't know what that meant for her, but the thought made ice skitter down my spine. I'd followed her to the mortal realm after I overheard Lukus suggesting she visit. His actions reeked of deception, and my suspicions were only confirmed when she was attacked. I watched in horror as those fae males dragged her through the dirt, disrobing her and saying such vile things. I was moments away from breaking my duties and stepping in.

Then Death had appeared.

A noise shook me from the memory, my body going rigid as I stopped short. I waited, hoping that my sisters would announce themselves, that it wasn't one of the deities lurking to catch us in our deceit. I'd felt safer somehow, when the Divine had been here. With her gone, though, it felt like nothing stood between us and the other gods.

"Sophia... Theora?" I called out into the void, my voice wavering with fear. No answer came and I started to retrace my steps, retreating up the hallway as what little courage I had gave way to cowardice. I made it one step, two steps, my racing heart starting to steady again as I thought perhaps my ears had played tricks on me. I took another deep breath, shaking my head to clear my thoughts and set my mind to venture back down the hall—just as something reached out and grabbed my wrist.

I opened my mouth to scream, terror ripping through me as I prepared to meet my end at the hand of whichever deity now had me. Another hand slapped against my mouth, trapping my scream in my throat.

"Would you *be quiet*, sister? Or are you trying to alert the whole palace as to our whereabouts?"

I breathed a sigh of relief as I recognized Theora's voice.

"Follow me, we don't have much time." Theora turned, keeping my hand in hers as she led me back down the hallway to a small alcove where I assumed Sophia was waiting. This deep within the palace, it was impossibly dark, too difficult to make out much of anything. But unless we wanted to give away our position, we'd have to make do in the dark.

"You're late," Theora hissed once she'd dropped my arm.

"Arne had me reorganizing a section of the archives and I couldn't get away. I think he was looking for something in our records." I looked over my shoulder to ensure the hallway behind me was empty.

"Were you followed?" Sophia's sweet voice was a rush of stark fear. Her worry mimicked my own unease. I was convinced Theora was the only one of us who was completely unafraid of what we were attempting. I shook my head in answer, only to realize she probably couldn't see the movement.

"Both of you have got to settle down," said Theora. "We won't succeed in anything if you give us away before we ever get a plan together."

I rubbed my arms, trying to get my body to settle as I let my sister's words wash over me. "I'm sorry, sister, it's just... aren't you scared of what they'll do to us if they find out?" I whispered as I threw another look over my shoulder, peering up the dark hallway for any sign of movement. Theora grabbed my shoulders, pulling my attention back to her.

"They won't find out." She leaned in, a gleam of torchlight reflecting briefly in her eyes, long enough that I could see the promised intent. Nothing but ravenous anger lay there. "Aren't you tired, Karmi? I know I am. We have lived our entire lives under their abuse and now—" Her voice dropped, the raw emotion of her pain slipping through. "They've harmed the Divine!"

I bristled, my eyes fluttering closed as I recalled the horrid moments in the mortal realm as Sophia tried to stifle a panicked gasp.

Perhaps she hadn't been attacked by their hand, but Lukus had sent her to the mortal realm intentionally, fully aware of how dangerous a journey it would be for her.

"They cannot get away with this treachery," Theora rasped. "This is just the opportunity we need. It's time for us to rise up. Time for us to stand up for ourselves, to step outside our duties and set aside our observations and documentation. Time for us to *do* something."

I held my breath. I had known the words were coming, but her voicing our greatest, most treasonous wish, here out loud in the depths of the palace was as terrifying as it was exciting.

Together my sisters and I watched over time and wisdom, a stewardship the gods had left to us as their scribes—when their interests fell to vanity and lust. Over the centuries, they had begun to abuse their power, delegating more and more work to me and my sisters while claiming more power for themselves and subjecting any lesser being—us included—to an existence more miserable than death. Perhaps it was time to take on one last responsibility. Perhaps it was time that we became the keepers of time and wisdom... and destiny.

"It's worth a try, isn't it, Karmi?" Sophia's voice was so soft, so pure—impossible to argue with. "For a chance to get out from under them? To do things better?"

I steeled my expression, pushing the fear and doubt far down within my mind, suffocating it until I was sure my eyes mirrored Theora's vengeful rage.

"Okay." The singular word pushed into the air, making everything around us go eerily still. A new chill ran over my skin as I thought of all my sisters and I had been through, of all that those of lesser power had been through across these realms, because of *them*. It was time for a change, time for a new world, a new regime. No matter the cost, no matter the risks. It was time for me and my sisters to end it.

"Okay," I repeated with more absolution. "Then let's make a plan."

CHAPTER 7
The Divine

The world around me took shape as I blinked awake. Darkness devoured me as I tried to make sense of where I was, the only light coming from a small candle beside me. My face pressed against whatever I lay on, and it took several moments of painful effort to get my hands under me to push myself up. The soft fabric slipped through my fingers, surprising me with its smooth texture. Silk. I pulled the ebony fabric around me, letting the candlelight reflect off the hypnotizing material.

My hands fell to my lap, running my fingers through the bedsheets absent-mindedly as I took in the rest of the chamber around me. Rough-cut stone made up the floor, the hearth, the walls—and pretty much everything else I could see. As if I was buried deep within some sort of cavern. There were no adornments to speak of, but rows and rows of books made up the far wall. In fact, books seemed to be strewn across the entire room, some in piles on the floor, placed in smaller stacks on a nearby table, or even spread across the sofa by the hearth.

I pressed my head to my hands, trying to focus on what I could remember. My mind was so fuzzy with the details of what had happened, how I ended up here. I wasn't even sure where *here* was.

Bits and pieces floated back to me: the atmosphere of the mortal realm, the images of bodies in cages, the vile look of the fae as he pinned me beneath him.

Had... Death been there?

I rubbed my forehead as pain bloomed behind my eyes, and let out a small groan. The noise felt deafening in the quiet of this space, and my blood quickly ran cold as it was returned by a deep growl, echoing from the far end of the room

I leaned forward ever so slightly, searching the room. A shadow moved just beyond the reach of the candlelight, formless and terrifying as two glowing red eyes looked back at me. I shrieked, slapping a hand over my mouth to stifle the sound as I shuffled back on the bed, pressing my back against the wall behind me.

"Ballam," a stern voice called out as I heard a door click shut. Death strode into the room, carrying what appeared to be a tray of food. "That's enough." The creature's growls subsided immediately as whatever it was retreated back into the darkness.

"You'll have to excuse Ballam, he's not used to having visitors down here." Death came up beside the bed I was perched on, still squeezing myself against the wall in fear.

"And Ballam is?" I asked, my throat still feeling raw from the attack with the fae. Death placed the tray of food on the bed before grabbing the candle and heading over to the hearth.

"My hound," he offered simply, not caring to expand on his explanation. Within a few moments, he had a fire blazing and returned to sit at the end of the bed. My eyes darted between the tray of food and the far end of the room where I could now see a massive beast sitting as still as stone beside the door.

"I promise it's not poisoned," he jeered, nudging the tray closer to me. I swallowed hard as I pulled my attention back to the deity sitting before me, unsure if it was wise to trust him. My stomach betrayed me, growling at the sweet smell of freshly baked bread wafting from the tray, and I grabbed it without another moment's hesitation. I broke into it, letting the steam rise to my face as I inhaled deeply. I sunk my teeth into the incredible texture, relishing the taste.

The corner of Death's lips ticked up as he watched me, making me suddenly self-conscious as I slowed my chewing. I'd never seen him so comfortable before, so... in his element.

Realization dawned on me, my hand going lax as I dropped the bread back onto the tray.

"Death..." Trepidation rang through my tone as I looked around the chamber again. "Where did you take me?"

A smug look settled across his face as he gestured around the room. "What's wrong, goddess? Never ventured down to the Depths before?"

Gooseflesh covered my skin as I recoiled. "I can't be here, Death."

"Cailli." Death's tone was even, calming—much to my surprise. "Eat. Rest. You have been through a lot tonight. Don't worry, I'll return you to your perfect little palace... in due time." He threw a wink my way.

My shock and horror turned red-hot as I fixed my glare on him. "No, Death. You will return me *right now*. You should know as well as I that our powers cannot coexist. I. Cannot. Be. Here."

A deep, steady growl reverberated through the shadows as the beast in the corner took a step forward. If it was possible to retreat further, I would have. The cold stone cut into my back as I pressed against the wall.

I reached out for my power, testing its strength in a place so opposite of the world I called home. It sparked to life in an instant, relief spreading over my chilled skin. Perhaps if it still worked down here, I'd be able to get back to the Realm of the Gods without needing his help.

"I hate to break it to you, Cailleach, but you don't have a lot of say in this decision." He backed off the bed, folding his arms across his chest as the beast came up beside him. "No one gets in or out of the Depths without my permission. And you need time to recover. When you have, we can talk more."

"Have you forgotten that I am the Divine?" I said, mustering up what little courage and strength I had left in me. "Darkness and death can lay no claim over the light of the living. It is your will which should submit to mine."

Death's lips set in a firm line as his gaze darkened.

"Perhaps you're used to how things go in your realm, but currently you are a guest in mine." He rose slowly, the sheer reach of his power forcing me to back down, eating through what little confidence I had left. "And trust me Cailleach, you'd know if I was claiming you. This is not that."

I stared at him, my mind reeling at his words, trying to unravel the mystery there. Bewildered by his meaning, I could do nothing more than gape as he retreated to the door on the other end of the room. The beast followed in his wake, taking up a spot beside the exit. He turned back to me for a moment, barely looking at me over his shoulder.

"This is nothing more than ensuring your safety." He paused, grimacing as he finally brought his eyes to mine from across the dark room. "A simple thank you would suffice."

And with that, he was through the door and into the world beyond, leaving me behind to my stone prison and the horrific guard dog to watch over me.

CHAPTER 8
The Divine

Time passed differently in the Depths. At least, that's what it felt like. There were no windows in this chamber, no sense of the outside world. I wasn't even sure if there *was* an outside world, or if the rest of this realm mirrored the endless stone covering the room that had become my prison. I passed the time with bouts of sleep and picking through the food Death continued to leave for me. He still would not hear my protests or pleas to return home, insisting I required further time to rest.

As much as I hated Death for keeping me here, it was hard to deny how it was helping me. My injuries from the attack had long since vanished, but that didn't stop the mental wounds from still bleeding. The thought of returning to the Realm of the Gods and facing the other deities after the horror I'd experienced... It felt shameful. I was a goddess, a deity of divine power, taken down by two lesser beings. It was impossible not to think about what would have happened to me had Death not found us. It was even more difficult to not think about what the other deities would think when they heard how defenseless I was, how stupid I'd been for going there alone and unprepared.

But with each passing hour, I felt that shame and guilt melt away. For whatever reason, his plan was working. As haunting as this room was, as much as I longed for the palace, my garden, and the warmth and beauty I'd worked so hard to cultivate, there was something about this place. Something intriguing and calming that was pulling me in and lulling me into a sense of security.

Once I was convinced the beast by the door wouldn't devour me for walking around the chamber, I ventured out to explore. I found a bathing room off to the side, much to my relief. But aside from that and a copious amount of books, there wasn't much else to see. A small wardrobe offered me a fresh change of clothes, albeit far too large. They were pure bliss compared to the tattered shreds of the dress that still clung to me, covering nothing.

I searched too for any method of escape. I stayed far away from the door, seeing as it was being guarded by the grotesque beast. But I searched every inch of the stone for any means of hidden passage—a crack or fissure that could give way to whatever lay beyond. I scoured the wardrobe, the bathing chamber, the shelves of endless books for anything that could be used for a weapon. I didn't know how to kill a being like Death, if he could even die. But perhaps stabbing him would give me the opportunity I needed to get away. If I knew how to summon the portal for the Realm of the Gods, I would have already been gone. While my magic worked here, I couldn't seem to get through the warding to the portal.

On my third pass through the wardrobe, I came across a discarded dagger within one of its drawers. I nearly squealed in delight, cutting a quick glance over to the beast at the door and hoping he wouldn't relay to his master what I'd found. I tucked the dagger within the folds of my oversized tunic, ripping a piece of the fabric to secure it to my side.

After another day had passed in this neverending prison, I started perusing the collection of books, desperate for anything to occupy me. Finding something that seemed vaguely interesting, I plopped down on the sofa by the fire and began reading. The pages pulled me in, captivating me in the tragic world within them, so much so that I didn't even notice when the beast made its way over to me. I stifled a scream as it sat at my feet, laying its head in my lap. This was the first time I'd seen it move outside of the times Death entered the chamber.

I looked down at the grotesque animal, my eyebrows raised as I held my hands back from where it leaned against me. I was scared to touch it, to move at all, for fear of it attacking. It must have noticed my hidden weapon, must have finally decided to take action against me for considering an attack against his master.

Moments passed as I stared at it resting against me. I swallowed hard, looking around the room for any sign of Death. Finding nothing, I turned my attention back to the beast. When he still didn't attack, I inched my hand slowly towards the top of its head, resting my palm between its ears...or were they horns? The sheer size if its head dwarfed my palm as it rested against it. Its skin felt leathery, hot and gnarled beneath my fingers. But I forced myself to pet it anyway, making sure to only move in calculated, gentle strokes.

The beast *whimpered*, the delicate noise sounding so at odds with the image of the vile creature before me. But within a moment its tail started wagging and it nuzzled further into my lap. A short sort of giggle broke past my lips, which only seemed to spur the beast on as it climbed on the sofa and curled up beside me. I hummed in assessment, trying to understand what had changed to make this animal suddenly like me.

"Well, I'm not going to argue with you," I said softly as I leaned into the beast, patting its head a few more times before opening the book again and picking up where I left off. I couldn't help the smile that broke across my lips as I read, thinking about the look on Death's face when he returned to see what had become of his big, bad guard dog.

I was halfway through my book—a particularly tragic love story about rival fae kingdoms and the star-crossed lovers that called them home—when the door to the chamber opened, startling me. The beast had long since fallen asleep, its snout cradled in my lap as I stroked its neck.

Death stopped short when he noticed his pet, rolling his eyes as he nudged the creature off the sofa. "What good is it having a depthhound when you're just going to turn on me the second I leave you alone with another deity?"

The beast let out a sound that was somewhere between a yawn and a growl, taking its time to stretch as it made its way back over to its station by the door.

"You didn't have to wake it," I protested. I let the book fall to my lap as I threw an accusatory glare his way. "We were having a rather nice time before you came in."

Death raised his eyebrows, taking the seat the beast had previously occupied. Being so close to him had me sitting up straighter, edging away to force more space between us. That familiar icy chill crept over me, as it did any time he got too close.

"*It* has a name. And Ballam is not a house pet. He's meant to guard and protect, not nap in the laps of pretty little deities giving him belly rubs."

I could feel the heat rise to my cheeks, unsure whether to feel flattered or insulted that he felt secure enough to comment on my looks. Refusing to acknowledge the remark, I turned back to my book and pretended to keep reading.

"I see you've made yourself at home with my books," he quipped, nodding toward the novel in my hand.

"*Your* books?" I asked, surprised.

"Of course, who else did you think they'd belong to?"

"Well," I stammered, trying to make sense of my own thoughts. "I guess I just assumed it was some sort of library for the Depths."

He chuckled, shaking his head. "No, Cailli, this isn't the sort of place that has things like libraries."

I rolled my eyes in frustration. "Okay, so why do you have this massive collection of books if this isn't *that sort of place*?" I leaned forward, gesturing for him to explain.

He considered me for a moment, huffing out something that sounded like another laugh as he said, "I get bored down here, I suppose. I took up a hobby." He shrugged, clearly uncomfortable with revealing details about himself, especially ones that threatened his reputation as the merciless Grimm.

I hummed in amusement as I watched his discomfort. "Well, you have good taste. I'll give you that much," I said, picking up the book I'd been reading and waving it before him.

He took it for a moment, running his fingers delicately over the fragile binding. "Yes, this one's a personal favorite." A soft expression flashed across his face as he looked over the book, almost as if to ensure its condition, before handing it back to me.

A moment of silence fell over us as I tried to wrap my mind around this suddenly new image of Death, tired and lonely down here by himself—finding ways to keep himself company with his books and his pets. I shook my head, the image far too absurd to let it linger any longer.

"How much longer are you going to keep me here, Death?" The dagger I'd found earlier burned against my side, reminding me of my initial plans to attack if he wouldn't let me leave. I wrapped my hands around my middle, running my fingers over the hilt through the fabric of my tunic. "I have duties to attend to back home. I need to speak with the other deities about—"

My words cut off, my mind flashing back to the conditions of that fae village and the countless mortals being held in their captivity. I could sense his eyes on me, the way his jaw flexed with irritation at the sudden change in conversation. There was a subtle uptick in the shadows that surrounded him as he debated his reply.

"You're free to leave at any time," he answered after several moments of silence. I whipped my head back to him.

"What do you mean, *I'm free to leave at any time*?" My tone was irritated as I turned fully to him, ready to fight. "You told me I was stuck here, that I couldn't leave without your say so. I've been wasting away down here, under the impression that I was at your mercy."

"I told you that no one gets in or out without my say so. Not that I wouldn't allow you to leave. I couldn't in good conscience allow you to leave while you were in poor health. Now that you're feeling better, it's your choice—no need for your valiant plans with that dagger you found."

I gaped at him, shock turning to irritation as a smirk settled across his face. How had he known about the dagger? I felt suddenly too exposed in front of him, as if every moment of my time here had been heavily monitored by him when I'd believed I'd been wholly alone.

I had no words to say, no argument to spit back. So instead, I just fixed him with a heated glare as I pulled the dagger from my side. I leaned forward, never breaking eye contact as I plunged it deep into the space on the sofa between us.

Death stifled a laugh, looking between me and the dagger now sticking out of the sofa. He waved his hand through the air, the dagger disappearing in a ripple of smoke and shadow.

"Why leave it for me to find?" I asked, finally piecing it together.

Death hummed, nodding slowly. "You're smarter than you look, goddess."

I rolled my eyes, irritated at his nonanswer. Death leaned forward, resting his elbows on his knees as he leveled his gaze at me.

"I wanted to see if you were capable of considering it. If you'd fight for yourself. For your freedom."

I scoffed, leaning back and folding my arms over my chest. "So did I pass your test?"

He mimicked my movements, leaning back into his spot on the sofa. He let his eyes drift over my form, making my skin crawl at the sudden attention. "We'll see," he finally answered when his eyes landed back on mine.

"Why do you hate us so much?" I asked finally. "What is so bad about us that you refuse to accept us as your own, that you'd take me and trap me down here to test me, just to see what I would do?"

His lips fell, a darkness weaving across his features. "For as long as I can remember, the other deities have considered me a villain. You hate me for the violence that is in my nature. For my duties and responsibilities amongst the realms."

He stood and walked over to the hearth, kneeling by the fire and spurring the wood to burn brighter. "Yet I didn't ask for this, I didn't make this choice. It's just what I am, what I exist to be. I have a cosmic role to play, just as you do, Cailleach. Just as they all do." He rose from the fire, dusting his hands before turning his attention back to me.

"It seems," he continued, crossing his arms as he leaned against the stone, "that I'm the only one who remembers that."

I looked down at my lap. Shame twined in my gut, suddenly recalling the conversation I'd had with Lukus. *When was the last time you visited the other realms?* At some point the other deities and I had locked ourselves away in the safety of our realm. But with the passing of time it had become harder and harder to remember why we thought that was a good idea. Death was right. We had long since abandoned our roles, perhaps me more than anyone else.

"But you're wrong," Death said, pulling me back from the thoughts circling my mind. I looked back at him, head cocked and brows furrowed. "I don't hate you. *Them*, maybe. But not you, Cailli. Never you."

I said nothing as I stared back at him in utter bewilderment. This god, this deity was the antithesis of my very being. Where I created, he destroyed. Where I shone, he infected with darkness. Yet he didn't hate me. And now, thinking back on the centuries past, I couldn't pinpoint a single reason I hated him either. Yes, his smirk was infuriating and his behavior towards me bothersome. He existed to consume the very things I created...but that was simply his duty, the balance of the realms. Had he ever truly been cruel? Had he ever given me a reason for my hate?

When push came to shove, I hadn't even been able to use the dagger against him. Something in me had hesitated, could not believe he was as vile and monstrous as the other deities claimed.

"I have something for you, when you're ready for it."

My ears perked up, his confession shaking me from where my thoughts had turned.

"For me?" I repeated, stunned. I couldn't remember the last time someone had given me a gift. But as I watched his face fall, his features going somber, I began to understand that perhaps I'd misunderstood what he'd meant.

"The fae." Death's voice had gone quiet, the room around us going dark as his shadows bled out from where he stood. "The one that harmed you. He's being held in one of my cells."

I tensed, trying desperately to ignore the feel of the fae's fingers on me, even here in the safety of Death's chambers days later.

"I just wanted you to know, before you returned to your realm." Death reached out, as if to console me, but let his hand drop midmotion. "He's yours, Cailleach. For whenever you're ready. To do with as you wish."

I shook my head fervently, adamantly declining the *gift* he offered. That was his duty, his business. No matter what the fae had done to me, I didn't have it in me to take his life.

Death watched me for a brief moment before averting his gaze to the fire beside him.

"I will not claim his soul. Not till you decide what you want his fate to be." His energy shifted, disappointment filling the space between us.

I couldn't help but feel like I'd just let him down. After his little test with the dagger, perhaps he had been led to believe I'd choose violence. But if it was bloodshed he wanted from me, then

I'd fail over and over again. I was not capable of it, not capable of destruction. My power was creation. He wanted something from me that I simply was not.

Yet something deeper longed for me to say yes, longed for me to exact my revenge for the way that fae had made me feel. Worthless, powerless. His actions had been blasphemous, stripping away my dignity and strength. That feeling of powerlessness still ravaged me, the desperate way I had called for my magic and it had been incapable of saving me—incapable of bringing light to that darkness. No, my power was not one of bloodshed. And if Death wanted him punished, he'd have to be the one to do it.

But I shoved those thoughts into the dark recesses of my mind, shaking my head in disgust of myself. No matter what the fae had done, no matter who was the one to claim his life, he was still my creation.

Death straightened suddenly. "Come on, goddess. I'll take you home," he said, moving through the room and back to the door. He didn't even wait for me to reply, didn't linger a moment longer than necessary as he motioned for me to follow him out into the Depths beyond. I rose to my feet, leaving the book behind as I moved to join him.

To my surprise, when we stepped through the threshold, it wasn't the Depths I found on the other side. My footstep landed in velvety grass, the sweet smell of peonies drifting to me from my gardens up ahead. I stood in wonder as I looked over my shoulder to see the doorway we'd just walked through. It shouldn't have surprised me, the ease in which he walked through realms—and yet I looked at him with wide eyes.

"Go on, Cailli. Return to your home. And for the hatred of all things holy, take the traitorous beast with you." As if in answer, the enormous beast came up beside me, nuzzling against my hand as he sat at my feet.

Death pivoted sharply to walk back through the doorway, the frame pulsing with pitch-black shadows.

"And a word for the wise," he said, lowering his voice to nothing more than a whisper. "I wouldn't share with the others what happened in the mortal realm."

"Why?" I asked, confused.

"Never give away your power, lest they use it against you." His words faltered for a moment, something that was completely out of character for him. "Look out for yourself. Because no one else will."

He stepped through the portal without another word, leaving me to the Realm of the Gods as the doorway faded in a shroud of inky black smoke.

Only the slightest inkling of his magic lingered in this realm. I stood there a moment longer, soaking up that feeling and realizing for possibly the first time ever that some part of me enjoyed the rush of his magic clashing against mine. Like inhaling a sprig of spearmint, or dipping in a brisk spring after spending my entire life in the sunlight.

The chilling tingle on my skin gave me a pleasant rush that intermingled with the eerie feeling creeping below my skin. What had his words meant? A shiver snaked its way down my spine as I turned towards the palace before me, concerned the lingering chill had more to do with what lay within those walls than it did with my time in the Depths.

CHAPTER 9
The Divine

My footsteps echoed off the palace walls, each reverberation reminding me how entirely empty it felt. The only other sound that greeted me was the steady clicking of Ballam's claws upon the marble floors as he followed in my wake. I must have only been gone for a matter of days, yet somehow this place suddenly felt so foreign to me, so hollow and unwelcoming.

I made my way towards the main sitting room, in search of the other deities. I hadn't come across anyone else so far and a tinge of dread was building deep within me. I needed to see them, to talk to them about everything that had happened. I hadn't told anyone where I was going and it dawned on me that they must have been sick with worry about where I'd been. Judging by the position of the sun, they were likely gathering for afternoon tea, as we often did.

I slowed my steps as the entryway came into view just up ahead. Death's warning to keep the attack from the fae between us rolled through my mind. I wanted to ignore his words, but I couldn't shake the knot in my stomach, nor the unsettled feeling I had remembering Lukus had been the one to suggest such a dangerous journey.

But surely the deities should know, given everything that was happening with the fae right now. An attack against a goddess was cause for concern. Actually, it would be grounds for war. I lingered just beyond the entry for the sitting room, suddenly unsure what I should do. I didn't want war. So much death already existed amongst the mortal realms. I didn't want their wrath to fall on the fae or any other beings of my creation.

But more than anything, I wasn't sure who I could trust. Perhaps Death was right. Perhaps it was best to keep that detail of my time away to myself—though that would make it harder to explain my absence. I took a deep breath, summoning as much composure as I could muster before turning the corner and stepping into the sitting room.

Estrid was perched upon a floral chaise by the open window, a small breeze filling the room with the smell of lilacs from the shrubs just beyond. She was buried in a book, probably some kind of romance novel. This room was Estrid's favorite. She'd claimed it as her own, decorating the place in every kind of flower imaginable. Lace lined the tables scattered throughout the room and satin pink curtains hung along the length of the walls, only breaking for the windows that opened to a small flower bed just beyond.

I still remembered the day she'd told me to plant them. I'd been so honored to help make this place something special for her—a sort of personal sanctuary. Just like I had done for myself in the gardens. She'd barely acknowledged them since that day, never even uttered so much as a thank you my way.

I watched her for a moment, the sun bathing her olive skin in golden light as she twirled a strand of her raven hair around her finger.

If there was ever a picture of a goddess, it was Estrid. She walked with power and purpose, maintaining an air of divinity in a way I was sure I never could. Even Lukus and Arne seemed to truly admire her, although I'm sure being the goddess of love and fertility didn't hurt in that area. All I knew was they never looked at me as they did her. All of them, in fact, seemed to have a certain respect for each other I was still trying to earn.

For as long as I could remember it had felt like there was Estrid and Arne and Lukus. And then there was me. It was hard to admit how badly I wanted to be a part of whatever it was they were. I felt so powerless beside them.

And then there was Death. I didn't even know how to begin to figure out how he fit into this picture. I was beginning to wonder if I didn't fit better cast into the Depths by his side than I did amongst this realm, beside the other deities.

I blinked, bringing myself out of my thoughts and tearing my gaze away from where Estrid sat. I cleared my throat quietly as I made my way fully into the sitting room. I sidestepped the various seating options—a collection of sofas in front of a thoroughly decorated hearth, a small sitting table with oversized, cushioned chairs—and finally found a seat close to her chaise. Ballam followed, curling up in the shadows of the room, his power extending the darkness to hide him from Estrid's sight.

"Oh, Cailleach, I didn't hear you come in." She stretched her arms out above her, letting the open book sit in her lap. I waited for her to ask where I'd been, if I was okay, but no such question came. Instead she offered me a half smile then returned to the book in her lap. "The boys should be here soon for afternoon tea, if you're looking for them."

"No," I answered quickly, a little jarred by her disinterest. "I just wanted to come apologize for my absence lately," I said finally, the words sounding awkward as they clambered off my lips.

"Hmm?" Her eyebrows rose slightly, her eyes never leaving the page of the book in her lap. "Oh yes, you haven't been around much, have you?"

Tears stung the back of my eyes, pained realization hitting me that Estrid perhaps didn't care about me as much as I had once hoped. I let out a slow breath as I blinked back the tears and smoothed out the too-big tunic I'd borrowed from Death's wardrobe.

Estrid's eyes finally left her book to look at me, her gaze raking over the foreign clothes in a condescending way. "What in the stars are you wearing?" Her face crinkled with disgust as she took me in, finally closing her book and sitting up a little straighter. I leveled my gaze at her, relieved that we at least were getting somewhere.

"That's what I'm trying to tell you, Estrid. I—" I stumbled over my words, trying to determine how to tell her where I'd been without revealing too much. "I've been with Death."

The mention of the God of the Underworld caught all of her attention as she swung her legs off the chaise and sat upright.

"Cailleach, why would you ever spend your time with that heinous monster?" She put a hand to her chest as a shiver ran through her body.

"He's not—" I started to argue, but the words died on my tongue. I didn't know what Death was. He'd helped me, yes. But I'd also seen him for the first time in all his terrible power when he'd killed that fae guard. And only the Cosmos knew what he was doing with the other one. "He was just helping me with something," I answered finally. My voice had dropped several levels, my confidence quickly fading.

Estrid eyed me, her gaze bouncing between my clothes and face. "Are you two..."

"Estrid! No!" I shrieked. I wanted to laugh at the absurdity, but the look of accusation and judgment on her face urged me to assure her that wasn't the case. "No," I said again, more firmly. "I just... I tried going to the mortal realms and I—got lost. He helped me find my way back home."

Estrid wouldn't stop staring at me, taking in every move I made, every emotion that was surely written across my face. I knew she didn't believe me. I wondered if she might push me on it, but she finally dropped her gaze, shaking her head.

"You need to be careful with him, Cailleach." Her voice dropped as she leaned in. "He's not safe."

"Who's not safe?" Arne's voice boomed as he entered the sitting room, Lukus following just behind. The sheer volume of his voice filled the room, making my teeth clench as I turned to face him. Ballam must have sensed my unease, because he was beside me in an instant, unleashing a deep, heated growl towards the males on the other side of the room.

"Fucking stars, Cailleach. What in the Depths is that?!"

Estrid jumped from where she'd been leaning towards me, shrieking in terror as she ran and hid behind the other deities.

"Is that—" Lukus made his way around Arne, taking a step closer to Ballam. Ballam let out another growl, baring his teeth as the three deities retreated a few steps.

"A depthhound, Cailleach? What the fuck is going on?"

I pressed my fingers to my forehead, pinching the bridge of my nose as I tried to think of a way to explain all of this. "Ballam," I ordered calmly. He immediately retreated, sitting beside me, though he watched the other three carefully as they stared in horror.

"As I was just telling Estrid..." I motioned to her now cowering form behind the two males. "My absence recently was due to some time away with Death. He was... helping me with something."

"Helping you with what?" Arne's face was red with rage, as he took a firm, powerful step forward. At Ballam's rising growl, Arne stood his ground—clearly ready to prove a point. But I noticed Lukus behind him, flinching and cowering as usual behind Arne while the God of Power did their dirty work. I suppressed the urge to smile at the god of war and mischief being held in his place by something as simple as a depthhound. Ballam was terrifying, but I would have thought it would take more to startle Lukus.

I paused, trying to decide how to answer his question. "We were investigating things in the mortal realms," I answered finally. "I wanted to see the carnage for myself, wanted to see what had become of my creation. Death was happy to oblige and helped me walk safely between realms. Were you aware just how bad things have gotten there? How much violence is rising?" I tensed as I waited for their response, feeling somewhat confident in where my story finally fell. As I was speaking, I noticed the sisters entering the sitting room, hastily setting up the afternoon tea and pretending they couldn't hear us.

"Of course, have we not been saying as such in our meetings?"

"It's more than that," I argued, my voice rising. "The land is wholly desecrated, the fae are doing vile, unspeakable things—"

"What would have compelled you to go to the mortal realm?" Arne cut me off, once again refusing to listen to my words. Anger welled within me. "How could you possibly think that is a good idea, given everything we've been dealing with lately?" Arne strained where he stood. His power vibrated through him, his body pulsing with the need to show his strength in some physical way.

I swallowed hard, my eyes finding Lukus'. He betrayed nothing, only waited as impatiently as Arne for the answer he already knew. I don't know why I expected him to speak up for me, why I expected any of them to listen to what I had to say. Still, it stung to be reminded of their lack of trust and respect for me. I felt myself retreat, my anger giving way for submission as Arne flexed his power before me. I averted my gaze, feeling suddenly so small before them.

"It matters not," Arne pressed on when I didn't answer. "You've more than proven that your sense of judgment and decision-making cannot be trusted. You must stay here, I will hear no more of these senseless journeys to the other realms."

I flinched at his insulting words, spoken with an authority he should not possess over me.

"And what of this?" Lukus took over the inquisition, gesturing carefully towards Ballam still beside me. Anger seethed inside me at his refusal to claim responsibility for urging me on that journey. If anyone had proven themselves untrustworthy, it was him.

I looked down at the animal, dutifully protecting me in the face of the deities' wrath. "Death left him with me," I answered timidly.

"Cailleach," Arne huffed out, rubbing a hand over his face, careful to keep one eye on Ballam. "You cannot just bring one of Death's mutations within our realm! He can't be trusted!"

"Is he not one of our own, Arne?" My voice was quiet as I let my question ring out through the room.

"Yes, but—"

"Then why are you so convinced he's a monster? He's filling his role, just as the rest of us must."

Arne blew out a breath of air so hot, I could almost see the steam coming off him. He eyed the depthhound one more time before stepping towards me. Ballam stayed put, listening to my order as I held my hand out to him.

Arne closed the distance between us, leaning down towards me so he was right in my face as he spoke. His golden hair curtained around his furrowed brows as he looked me in the eyes. "There's a difference between fulfilling your role, and reveling in the darkness that it requires."

His words were ominous, hanging in the air for a long time after he spoke them. Visions of Death ripping into that fae male flashed in my mind. The smile on his face as he watched the male's lifeless body fall to the ground, the joy he took in making the other one scream in terror as he was forced to kneel in the blood of his friend's corpse.

"You've seen it, haven't you? You know exactly what I'm talking about." Arne shook his finger at me as he watched me recall the horrors I'd witnessed that night in the mortal realm. He clapped his hands together once as he walked back towards the others. "That right there, that's why you need to keep your distance. Why we *all* must stay away from him. He is a threat to our existence."

Arne patted Estrid on the arm, taking her hand gently in his own and leading her to the sofas where the sisters had finished setting up the tea. "He may be a deity, but he is not one of us." His eyes shot back to me as he settled into his spot on the sofa, Estrid tucked securely beneath his arm. "And it would do you well to remember that."

I hummed as I made my way across the room to where they all sat. Taking a seat on the opposite side of the low table, I grabbed one of the delicate cups and poured myself some of the steaming tea, the familiar tart and fruity aroma stinging my nose.

"And why is that?" I asked finally, stunning Arne. I picked at a piece of shortbread, waiting for him to answer.

"Because Cailleach," he finally responded after a beat of silence. "The last thing we need is for the Divine to start associating with Death. You are creation, and he is destruction. Pure and simple. We need you to remain pure, we need your power to remain intact. Just as you said, we all have a role to fill. And if Death starts challenging your power, corrupting it or affecting it in any negative way... well, it would make it quite difficult for you to fill your role. And then what would we do with you?" He raised his teacup at me, throwing a wink my way.

I leaned back in my seat, bringing my own teacup to my lips and attempting to hide the way my hands shook as a chill crept down my spine. My eyes darted around the room, desperate to find anything to look at besides Arne's cold stare. Karmi was just beyond the sofas, collecting the last of the trays they'd brought the afternoon tea in with. Her eyes caught mine with a somber weight as I sipped from my cup. Something akin to dread coursed through my veins and was mirrored in her eyes as she dipped her head to me and scurried out of the room.

CHAPTER 10
Death

I sat in the solitude of my private chambers, the chambers Cailli had occupied during her short time with me. I'd wanted more than anything to show her the rest of my realm, the kingdom I'd built here. But I knew she wasn't ready for that yet. I ran my hand along the midnight satin bedding, relishing in the warmth that still lingered in the sheets from her power. Watching her walk back into that den of vipers had been nearly impossible. Letting her go when I was so close to claiming everything I ever wanted was even harder.

I sucked in a deep breath through my nostrils, eyes closed as I clung to the very essence of her soul that still permeated the air. I followed that trace between realms, reaching out in my mind to Ballam. Opening my eyes once more, it was not my private chambers I saw around me but hers. The Divine.

Ballam trailed behind her, on guard for any unwanted followers. I could feel the muscles in his ears twitching as if they were my own as he strained to listen for any suspicious sound. I could tell in the way Cailli walked through her chambers that she was exhausted, her shoulders hung low, her eyes drooped as she trudged through the vast room to her wardrobe on the other side.

After a moment of prodding through the drawers, she produced a sleeping gown and disappeared into the bathing chambers to prepare herself for bed. She clicked the door shut behind her with one last lingering look to Ballam. As she dressed for bed, I spoke into Ballam's mind, giving him careful instructions for what I wanted him to do. He paced the chamber as I spoke, checking the space for anything suspicious.

Ballam had been my first creation, my closest and only friend over the centuries of isolation. I trusted him with anything. But my shoulders still tensed because I couldn't be there to defend her myself. I knew it was only a matter of time before they banished the depthhound and I'd lose sight of her altogether.

The deities might say they wanted to put an end to the increased death tolls, but I'd begun to discover their true intentions I was still piecing my theories together, still walking the realms to find more information on who was behind all of this, but I knew there were more sinister schemes unfolding amongst the Realm of the Gods than they'd ever admit.

Cailli was so innocent, so naive. I knew how desperately she wanted to be a part of the other deities, to live in harmony with them and be considered a peer, an equal. If only she knew how much more she was capable of. She didn't belong with them, but not because she wasn't good enough. Because she deserved so much better. I just had to make sure I could keep her protected until she remembered that for herself.

I urged Ballam to the door while the goddess was occupied in the bathing room, letting my shadow magic slip out through the hound and ease the door to the hallway open. He stepped out into the dark, vacant hall and made his way quickly through the palace. I enveloped him in shadow as he walked, softening the click of his claws and the weight of his presence as he did my bidding. It didn't take him long to find what I was looking for.

Ballam's cloaked body slunk through the deep stone archives. I held him back as one of the sister's finished her records for the day, filing away the parchment amongst the walls of scrolls and slipping out into the hall. The room darkened as shadows drifted over parchment, whispering their findings to me. This place was full of information, centuries of recordkeeping by the sisters. That was their duty as scribes to the gods. And as such, it was impossible for me to request any scrolls on what I needed to know, even harder to come peruse the archives myself. Doing either would risk giving away that the deities' hold on my memories was slipping.

Over the centuries I'd scoured archives throughout the realms, more tomes than I could count, feeling deep down like the answers had to be inside them. Why I always yearned for her, why I hung on every golden word. And now I was closer than ever in proving it, in confirming a world in which we had always been good for one another, a world in which Death and Life had once been intertwined.

I knew the information I needed wouldn't be easy to find—damn near impossible if any of them found out what I was looking for. Conveniently though, the archives weren't far from Cailli's chambers and leaving Ballam with her had proved to be beneficial in more ways than one. It would take multiple visits to finish our search, especially without anyone noticing Ballam's absence.

Murmuring voices drifted down the hallway, pulling our attention from the walls of parchment. My shadows pulled back, lifting the darkness that had fallen over the room until only Ballam was covered. He retreated from the archives, following the muffled sounds to a small chamber where the other deities were huddled together, whispering in the cover of night.

"What are we going to do?" Estrid's voice squeaked through the night.

"Would you calm down, Estrid? She's not going to find out *anything*. We just have to keep them separated. And get rid of that damn depthhound."

I watched through Ballam's eyes as Arne put his hands on Estrid's shoulders, forcing her to stop fidgeting. Lukus was beside them, perched on the window seat, deep in thought. Of the three, I knew Lukus was the more problematic one. Arne was stronger, but it was a brute kind of strength. He didn't know how to wield it wisely. Lukus, though—he was a schemer. It's why Arne still used him. He knew he needed Lukus's mind, while keeping him in check with his power. And by rewarding him with Estrid's attention.

"Death thinks he can come into our realm and spy on us, but he underestimates us." Lukus finally turned his face back to the others, a wicked smile curling across his lips. "He may be the Ruler of the Underworld, but I'm the God of War and Mischief. He overstepped by allowing a depthhound in our realm. I think it's time we remind him where he belongs."

Arne mirrored his smirk as he let out a dark chuckle, clapping a hand on his back. "I couldn't have said it better myself, Lukus. And if it pushes them further apart in the process, well, that's just an added bonus."

Arne guided the two of them down the hall to where I assumed his chambers were located. The grit of their murmurs eventually turned into distant moans of pleasure, turning my stomach as I confirmed my suspicions about the true details of their entanglement. Lingering for one more moment in the seething hatred that surrounded me, I urged Ballam swiftly back down the halls and into Cailli's chambers just as she slipped back into the main room.

"And just what are you doing?" she asked Ballam as she looked between him and the open door. She padded on bare feet over to him, the soft olive material of her sleeping gown swaying around her body. She patted his head gingerly and peered out in the hallway before closing and locking the door. "Best to stay close to me, boy. The others aren't thrilled about you being here. I'd hate for you to end up alone with one of them. They may..." She trailed off as she walked around the room, extinguishing the lit candles. I could hear the fear in her voice, could see it in the muscles tensing across her face and back. She finally finished her turn around the room, tucking the key to the door in the drawer of an end table.

She froze as she turned to the bed, noticing the small rectangular shape tucked carefully against her pillow. She picked it up, looking back to Ballam—to me. My face softened as I watched her turn the book over in her hand. Her mouth gaped open, inspecting it carefully as she climbed into bed.

"Did you know about this?" she asked Ballam, finally. He came up beside her bed and sat at attention as she ran her fingers delicately over the pages, finding the note I'd left inside. She pulled out the piece of parchment, her eyes tracing the ink on the page as I recalled the message I'd left for her:

I said it was one of my favorites. Not that you couldn't take it with you. What good is a favorite book if I have no one to discuss it with? –Death

She stared at the paper far longer than it took to read my note. So long, in fact, that I began questioning if perhaps I'd made a mistake. Sneaking into her room after I'd brought her back to this realm was a risky chance to take. I knew it was an invasion. Perhaps it scared her—knowing that Death had been amidst her private quarters, had walked her halls. My shoulders tensed as I ridiculed myself for making such a foolish mistake. In a single decision I'd wrecked every bit of progress I'd made with her. It was too risky, too stupid.

Her face split into a wide grin as she made some sort of alarming noise akin to a laugh. She clutched the book tight to her chest as she sunk into the bedding and cracked open the pages from where she'd last left off. She shot a look back to Ballam, suddenly embarrassed by her outburst.

"Please don't tell him I did that," she begged. The air was charged with her power, the giddiness radiating off her as she dove into the novel.

I breathed out a long, slow breath as I let myself finally relax. I was so sure I'd screwed this entire thing up, but seeing her so happy—feeling so safe—after the chaos she'd endured recently... it did more to warm my spirits than anything had for decades. Centuries, even.

"Keep her safe, Ballam," I ordered. *"I'll be back soon to search further."* My consciousness slipped back into my own body, my own realm. I blinked my eyes as her chambers faded away and the familiar surroundings of my library greeted me. It was empty, cold, as I stood and paced the small space. I ran my fingers over the collection of books I'd built for myself over the centuries. My prized possession—my only possession, really. Aside from Ballam and my other mutations. And the souls that filled the Depths, though most days I wished otherwise. But these books—they were the closest I'd come to finding joy in my lifetime. Pages filled with imaginary lives I could have lived, if only the cosmos had decided differently.

But with her, I could have a life like that. I'd sacrifice every book amongst the realms if it meant having her in my arms. I'd burn every last page of prose and vow to never read again if it meant living a life with her by my side. Because seeing her tonight, feeling that joy and power and *strength* radiating off her—that had brought more joy to my cold heart than any book ever could.

CHAPTER 11
Karmi

Tensions were high in the palace after the Divine's return. I trusted Theora and her plan, even if she wasn't sharing it fully. But with each passing day it seemed as if we were even further from achieving our goal. I supposed discord amongst the gods was in our favor. It was something to keep them distracted, for now. But the way my sisters and I had to duck out of sight for fear of being at the receiving end of their wrath made me feel even smaller than usual.

Still, Theora was confident that we were on track. She whispered such reassurances to me as we worked in the kitchen, preparing breakfast for the deities. Other servants bustled around us through the kitchen, the souls claimed worthy enough to enter the Realm of the Gods. If only they'd known what they'd been considered worthy enough for. Their afterlife was nothing more than bondage to this realm, a mindless, will-less eternity of servitude to the gods.

I couldn't look at them for long without feeling pity and shame. I peeked over my shoulder as they drifted through the kitchen, dropping off a load of dirtied dishes and meandering back out the door for whatever was demanded of them next. Looking back down at my hands, elbow-deep in a fresh batch of dough for a breakfast I wouldn't even get to eat, I was suddenly aware how similar we were. While the indentured souls had no ability to resist, we at least had our minds and our power. I kneaded the bread with a new sense of anger as Theora continued whispering the next round of plans into my ear.

"Lukus has requested my presence in his chambers this afternoon." Theora didn't take her eyes off the berries she was mashing as she spoke. I knew if she looked at me, I'd find shame in those dark blue eyes.

I gritted my teeth in disgust at the idea of that vile creature touching my sister. I'd been there plenty of times after Lukus's *visitations*. I knew how he left her. And I was often the one that pieced her back together, especially after particularly rage-filled sessions.

He'd wanted Sophia, but Theora had convinced him to lie with her instead. It was only a matter of time before that desire would no longer be sated. Especially if Arne caught wind of Lukus's yearnings. Everything between them seemed to be some sort of competition, a battle for power.

"The deities are rather displeased with the presence of a depthhound amongst the Realm of the Gods," continued Theora. "Perhaps my visit will provide an opportunity to pry some, give me a chance to search his chambers or press him for information."

I tightened my fists as I pushed harder into the dough, kneading with more force than necessary. "Theora," I started to argue, "you don't need to—"

"I do," she answered firmly, a warning in her tone. We both knew what would happen if she denied him. I looked over to where Sophia was on the other side of the kitchen, filling a basin of water to wash the large pile of dishes beside her.

Theora sighed in frustration as she finally turned from the muddled fruit to look at me. "There is much discord amongst the deities after Cailleach's time with Death. We need to exploit that if we want any kind of chance at bringing them down. Pushing to further that conflict will only help us in the long run."

I quickly averted my gaze as I tried to hide my confusion. "This just all feels like overstepping our duties, Theora. We're meant to observe only. To record. I'm just worried what might happen if—" Theora sighed again, cutting me off by laying a hand on my arm to stop my work.

"I know this is all hard for you and Sophia to follow. But please just trust me. The less you know the better. There are things I can see that you cannot." She offered me a hard smile. "Remember that our powers manifest in different ways," she added, removing her hand from my arm and tapping her temple.

I knew she was right. Theora was the oldest, the wisest, and the watcher. She connected things that Sophia and I never could. It's what made it so easy to trust her. But it hadn't come without its repercussions. Theora's mind had become burdened with a weight neither Sophia or I could understand. Part of me had begun to worry for Theora, her sanity seemingly threadbare some days. It had me questioning the path she was leading us down, if she truly understood the risks and consequences if things didn't go our way.

Theora had returned to her task and seemed to have moved on from the conversation. She was gone within a moment, checking in on Sophia before adding the berry mixture to a pot over the fire. I finished the dough with a few more rough kneads and left it to rise as I gathered a tray for tea. I knew at least some of the gods would be in the sitting room by now, waiting for their morning tea—and if they didn't get it soon, I'd be scolded for making them wait.

Pushing out of the kitchen and across the hall into the open sitting room, I was surprised to only find the Divine there. She was reclining on a sofa by the window, that hideous beast curled up beside her as she read from a book I didn't recognize. I moved to the main table, setting down the tray and preparing a cup for her.

"Good morning, Karmi," the goddess chirped as she put her book down. The beast raised its head to look at me but lowered it again into the Divine's lap. Seeing her befriending such a vile creature was perplexing. Her essence was so contrasting to that of the beast. I shook my head, realizing that I was staring as the Divine waited for my reply.

"Good morning, Your Grace. I have your tea ready, if you'd like it?"

The Divine rose, padding on bare feet over to the table. "Oh, you didn't have to do that. I could have made it myself."

My eyes darted around the room, confused by her insistence. I couldn't remember the last time one of the deities made their own tea, even the Divine. "I just wanted to be sure it was ready before the others requested it." The Divine followed my gaze around the empty room before leaning in towards me.

"I think the other three are still preoccupied." It was hard to miss the note of contempt in her voice as she took her cup and plopped in an extra sugar cube. "They aren't particularly in favor of Ballam. They've been avoiding me since my return."

My eyes quickly fell to the beast who had followed her over to the table. I almost jumped in surprise to realize how close he was, how silent he'd been in his approach. My heartbeat quickened as I took in the state of him: leathery black skin where fur should have been and ears that curled upon his head like a pair of horns. A thing of nightmares. I retreated a few steps back, under the guise of straightening the floral arrangement on the table.

The Divine smiled as she stirred her tea. "He won't hurt you, Karmi. He's really such a sweetie, once you get to know him."

I eyed the beast, then her, entirely unconvinced at her reassurance.

"That is," she added as she took a sip from her cup, "unless you're a threat to me."

My head snapped back to her, ice creeping down my spine and through my veins as I gaped, speechless. "I—no, Your Grace, I would nev—"

The goddess broke out into a small giggle as she reached out and grabbed my hand. "Calm down, Karmi, it was just a joke." I let out a hot, anxious breath as I pretended to laugh along with her, sucking down air to calm my body. "Truthfully Karmi, you've been more of a friend to me than anyone else here in such a long time. I wanted to thank you for that kindness. If there's anyone I can trust, I think it's you."

I forced a tight smile, bowing my head to her. "Of course, Your Grace. I'm always here for anything you need." I began retreating from the room, desperate to be done with this interaction.

"Would you like to join me for a walk through the gardens later today? It's such a nice day outside and I'd love to show you the plants I've been working on recently." She turned her head to the open window, looking with longing towards the gardens. "They've turned out quite stunning, and I'd love to share them with someone."

I shook my head hesitantly. "I'm sorry, Your Grace, but I have duties I must attend to."

Her gaze fell, nodding in understanding. "Of course, I'm sorry—I should have thought of that. Forgive me."

A moment of silence fell between us as she fidgeted with a doily on the tray.

"I would love to see them," I finally offered, taking one small step forward. "Sometime."

Her eyes found mine once more, kindness and sorrow swirling in them. The weight of her loneliness was tangible, cracking the wall I was trying desperately to build between us.

"Okay," she said, nodding eagerly as I offered her a small, reassuring smile.

"Okay," I agreed.

And with that she turned back to her perch in the corner, the depthhound following at her feet. I scurried out of the sitting room without another moment of hesitation, rushing down the hall and out of sight as my heartbeat thrummed in my ears. Once I was sure I was truly alone, I dipped into an alcove and leaned against the solid wall for support. Pressing a hand to my heart and another to my head, I forced deep, greedy breaths into my lungs. It took me several minutes to gather my bearings and calm my racing heart.

I thought for certain she'd discovered our plot, my mind reeling from the possibility of her finding out the truth... let alone one of the other deities. I swiped at my eyes, tears and sweat both running down my face. No matter the empathy I felt for her, no matter the kindness she offered me, I needed to keep my distance. I couldn't let her get close. If she uncovered these secrets, if she knew what we had planned before it was time, it could ruin everything.

I slowed my breaths, straightening after several moments of reprieve. With one last focused breath, I collected myself and took off down the hall with a renewed focus.

CHAPTER 12
Death

The darkness of the mortal realm surrounded me as I stalked through what was left of the forest. I had no desire to be out amongst the mortal realm tonight, no desire to be filling my time with such violence when I was on the verge of revealing everything I'd been working towards.

But I was bound by duty, so when duty called...

I slowed my movements, watching the small figure up ahead. She was flighty, scurrying around with wide eyes and hunched shoulders as if she didn't want to be seen. I didn't know what had brought her to the mortal realms, but I could smell her fear from here. My shadows inhaled it deeply, stretching and growing at the tease—desperate for more.

I stepped out of the darkness, revealing myself to her. She jumped, momentarily losing control of her composure, and slapped a hand over her mouth to mute the squeal I knew was building in her throat.

"Your Grace," she squeaked.

"Please explain, Karmi, why you're out here walking the mortal realms. Alone." She shifted, sliding whatever package she carried behind her back. My eyes tracked the movement, wondering what a scribe of the gods could possibly be hiding within the shadows of a forest in the mortal realms. My power bristled, my shadows whispering to me of the promised possibilities that package could hold—perhaps even the missing piece I'd been searching for to finally reveal the truth to Cailli.

"And what is that?" I could feel the power emanating from it, calling to me as if it was speaking to my very soul. My jaw clicked in irritation as she tried to evade my question.

"I wasn't aware you'd been called to the mortal realms tonight, Your Grace. Please forgive me. I would not have ventured out if I knew I'd be interfering with your work." She shrunk back again.

"Death," I corrected. "Drop the formalities, they mean nothing to me."

She stopped, eying me cautiously, as if to decide if she believed me, before correcting herself: "Forgive me, Death."

I crossed my arms, setting my jaw as I looked down on her. "I'm waiting."

"I don't—, I'm not sure—" She took another step back.

I rolled my eyes, throwing out a hand to wrap my shadows around her and hold her in place. The power inside me was taking control, forcing out a darker side of me I normally didn't care for. But at the moment, I couldn't find the energy to be bothered. Not when there was a very real possibility she held the one thing within her grasp that I'd spent centuries searching for. When the stakes were as high as this, I didn't have time to be amiable.

"Wait!" she cried out. But I didn't listen. If she was hiding what I thought she was, I would do anything required to pry it from her hands.

"The other deities are lying to you!"

Her shouts stopped me—the darkness of my magic rooting me to the spot, crawling over my skin and screaming to be fully released. Within mere moments I was on her, towering over her with my hand wrapped around her throat.

"Lower your voice," I seethed. My gaze shot past her, peering into the surrounding area. I sent out a wave of shadows to search for any listening ears.

Karmi's eyes went wide. "You know?"

"I know enough," I answered, once my shadows had returned to me. Lowering my voice, I leaned down to her ear. "And I know that the realms are full of prying eyes and ears. And you're a fool for being so careless."

She swallowed nervously, her blue-green eyes peering up at me in fear. I released my hand but held my position over her.

"I'm scared, Death," she confessed. "Theora has been re-searching, looking for ways to go up against them. But she was worried they were getting too suspicious." She diverted her gaze, staring at the small piece of rugged forest floor between us. "That's why she sent me here."

"To do what?" I asked through gritted teeth.

She thought for a moment, chewing on her lip as her eyes darted around us. As if she had any other option besides answering me.

"To hide something she'd finally found, hidden amidst the God of War and Mischief's chambers."

She produced the package from where she'd hid it behind her back, pushing it towards me in haste.

"Take it."

My brow rose, honest surprise washing over me and dampening the frustration that had taken hold. My fingers curled around the suede sachet that covered the item inside. I knew what it was, even through the thick material that obscured it from view.

The missing tome from the archives. The final piece of the puzzle. Our true origin story.

"Theora won't share her plan with us. But I know she's planning something. She wanted me to bring this here and hide it amongst the mortal realms, assuming the deities would never brave a visit here to find it." The trepidation was clear in her voice.

"But you're giving it to me instead?" I pushed.

She nodded hesitantly, risking a glimpse in my eyes. "I'm concerned for Theora. And I want to be sure there's contingencies in place... She hasn't seemed in her right mind as of late—she's been too secretive, too withheld inside her own mind."

"Explain."

A battle waged behind Karmi's eyes, a hidden struggle to decide if she trusted me or not.

"Our minds are filled with the realms' records. We keep physical records as well, of course." She gestured to the book I was clutching against my side. "But the archives exist first and foremost in our

minds. And if we aren't careful about managing that burden…
it can take over.

"She's spent centuries receiving the brunt of the deities'
abuse. That's a long time to let bitterness fester. And the way
she's been talking as of late—I just don't want her to end up
doing something drastic, something she'll end up regretting."

"By the Depths," I breathed out, letting my face fall as I
scrubbed a hand over my head. The last thing we needed was
a deranged scribe attempting to take on Arne. He'd crush her
without a second thought. And there was no doubt in my mind
the action would put him on our trail, if he wasn't already.

"Okay, Karmi, listen carefully." I let my shadows grow, taking
extra care that we were guarded. They wrapped around us and
entwined over the book in my hand, obscuring it from view
completely. "Return home. Do all that you can to stay out of
the deities' path. But don't divert from your normal routines.
They can't know I found you. That you gave me this." I dipped
my head down towards the tome now covered completely in
shadows. "Tell your sisters what you must, but you cannot take
on the deities on your own."

I felt my shadows tug at me, a wandering soul lingering
somewhere close by.

"I will take care of the Divine. And I will figure out a way to
bring them all down."

"But how?" Karmi's eyes went wide with desperation. It
struck a foreign feeling in me—something like pity.

"I can assure you," I growled. "The Divine is safe with me. Return home. Let me worry about the others. But if anything further develops, summon me here." I turned to walk away, but Karmi followed, more desperate pleas breaking through the silence of the night. She'd lost her composure again, unaware of how loud her voice carried—unaware of the creature my shadows had captured just beyond the trees.

I spun around, letting my presence overtake her. The mask of Death slipped in place as my shadows surrounded her.

"I said return home, *lesser*."

My words radiated through the trees with the weight of my power. Even as I heard the words leave my tongue, a small part inside of me cringed. But if she wouldn't listen then I would *make* her listen. I would make her understand that we were not a team, that I was not here to help her.

Karmi fell backwards. The hurt and shock from my words was evident. But I hardened my heart, refusing to let it crack for the being in front of me. I needed to keep my mind focused on one thing and one thing only: protecting Cailli. I finally had my opportunity to claim her and I would be damned if anything got in the way of us again.

My shadows reined in, bringing with them the creature they had found within the trees, a measly fae being. Most wouldn't have given him a second look, but I was not most. I knew the dangers of underestimating others, especially those who had spent their lives at the end of violence and despair. Pain made people do crazed things. Desperate, depraved things. And just as I wouldn't let myself trust the sisters, I wouldn't let this insignificant fae get away.

Karmi watched in horror as the cries of the fae grew closer, as my shadows dragged him through the rotted filth of the forest floor. Her eyes flickered from the rippling shadows stretched out across the ground like an obsidian mist, back to my face. She clutched her chest, slowly creeping further and further away

"Run along now, Karmi. Unless you'd like to help me rectify your carelessness."

She shook her head adamantly as she turned and began to run.

"Good," I called out, knowing she was too far to hear my words. "You wouldn't have the stomach for what comes next anyways."

The pitiful creature landed at my feet, bound in my shadows. He was screaming and trembling, reeking of piss and shit. My shadows rejoiced—their hunger strong tonight, desperate to lash out after all Karmi had shared.

Perhaps he would have wandered on, not thinking twice about the two beings he saw huddled in the forest discussing oddities he didn't quite understand. But I couldn't take the chance. I couldn't let him go when there were too many things out of my control as it was. I wouldn't risk him reporting back to someone in the fae kingdoms. The deities didn't pay much attention to the mortal realms, but a report such as this would be enough to catch their eye, especially now.

I couldn't let something so simple and careless get in the way of my intentions with Cailli. I couldn't endanger her so. I reached my hand out to the sniveling, terrified creature at my feet and let my shadows constrict around his body.

His screams were cut off, his eyes bulging as his skin turned a deep shade of red. I watched with indifference as my magic pulled the air from his lungs and my power squeezed the life out of his pathetic body.

I had so much rage built up within me. So much anger and hatred stored up for the deities that had kept me from my goddess. After everything Karmi had shared, after everything I'd found out for myself...all that rage had to go somewhere. I'd been denying it for so long, playing the tactful role necessary to keep my discoveries under wraps. But now, with this tome in my hand, with nothing but a doorway between realms and a bit of magic keeping me from revealing all to my goddess, I couldn't help the dam that broke free within me. It flooded me with all those long suppressed emotions, endless pain and bitterness.

I leaned down, bending over the fae clinging to his last moments.

"Unfortunate night for you," I mused, patting his cheek as streams of blood now coated his skin from the dripping orifices of his face. I stood, stepping over the body and letting loose a breath from the sudden relief of tension that had been steadily building in my veins.

With the missing tome from the scribes tucked safely in the crook of my arm, I flicked my other hand to the body behind me. With that simple motion, my shadows were set free, rushing what was left of the fae and devouring him, body and soul. With them came a freeing sensation, the burden of that rage and power suddenly lighter than it had been in centuries.

I threw my arm out before me, revealing the doorway to the Depths and stepped up to the threshold. I turned around for one last look, adjusting the collar of my tunic as I watched my shadows at work. Pursing my lips together, a sharp whistle broke through the trees, calling my shadows back to me in an instant, fully fed and content. I marveled at the sensation, letting my gaze pore over the mortal realm one last time before stepping back into the Depths. It was time to go claim my goddess.

CHAPTER 13
The Divine

Days passed without hearing a word from Death. I'd thought with his depthhound here, he'd be more apt to check in. I supposed that was the point though, leaving Ballam here so he didn't have to waste time checking on me unnecessarily. I debated trying to reach out to Death through the depthhound, but couldn't find the gumption to actually try. It wasn't like I needed him. I'd recovered from the attack just fine. And even though the memories lingered in the form of nightmares, I was truly doing well—all things considered.

I'd found a certain amount of joy in the time since my return, falling back into my normal routine amidst the other deities. Though I'd been hesitant when Death insisted on leaving Ballam with me, the hound and I had grown quite fond of each other in our short time together. I leaned over, running my hand down the length of his back as we walked towards the gardens. He leaned into my touch, nudging his head into my side. I grinned at the affectionate move.

Having him with me through the night, a comforting presence and reminder of safety, had done more to ease my mind than I thought it would. When the thoughts swirled of who I could trust, or what pieces of the puzzle I was missing, Ballam was there to help me feel safe and grounded. When I woke up shaking from the memory of that fae male hovering over me, his magic twining around me, Ballam was the one to calm me.

The first night it happened, he climbed up in my bed without hesitation and curled up against me. He laid his head on my chest and stayed until my breathing returned to normal and my shaking settled. There were some nights I woke to him pacing the room or seated by my locked door, as if he had sensed something on the other side. But he never hesitated to come back to me once I'd woken to cuddle up beside me and lull me back to sleep.

I hadn't seen much of the others since that first interaction when I'd come home. They seemed to make themselves scarce any time Ballam and I stumbled upon one of them. The sisters even seemed busier than usual, as unfathomable as that seemed. Karmi couldn't even spare a moment away to go to the garden. I wondered if the gods had become more demanding in my absence, or if somehow the passage of time had quickened its pace.

The palace had become a terribly isolating place, even with the company of the depthhound. I'd grown used to the solace this realm offered, cherished it even. But ever since my return, I couldn't enjoy it as I once had. It felt too lonely, too quiet, and I found myself wondering what had changed. Arne's words still haunted me, too. A promise to take action not only against Death, but me as well if it came to it.

I shook my head, pulling my thoughts back to the present as we walked through the wrought-iron archway of the garden. I released the latch to the gate, letting my fingers run over the metal spikes. It was an intricate design, swirls of black curving and winding up to form an arch of stars and suns. Deep green vines wove their way through the iron, forming a small canopy that offered us reprieve from the blazing light of the setting sun.

The garden was bursting with life, a private collection of all my personal favorites that nature had to offer. Peonies bloomed in excess, their abundance looking akin to the thick cotton clouds that hung in the sky above. A wall of jasmine lined the back of the garden, surrounded by hyacinth and honeysuckle. Colors of every hue greeted me as I took a turn, reveling in the beauty I had created here.

I made my way through the rows of life, finally stopping at my new addition. It was a secret project I'd been working on since returning home, a unique kind of plant that only bloomed at night. It had been so long since I'd created something entirely new. I almost forgot how freeing it could feel. I kneeled beside the dark stalks, pruning the plants as I waited patiently for the sun to finish setting.

Before long, the moon replaced the sun and the night came to life with the chirping of crickets and the soft glow of fireflies. I sat back, resting my palms against the warm grass and soil, and watched my new creation come to life. Blossoms unfurled in the moonlight, their obsidian petals nearly indistinguishable in the cover of night. Just as the bloom opened itself to the world, a small silver orb rose, casting the flowers in their own little beams of moonlight.

The petals lit up beneath the silver glow, their opposed textures somehow irresistibly intertwined. The outside of the petals were thick and leatherlike—for Ballam, my newfound protector and companion. The insides, though, were soft as silk—for the feel of Death's silk sheets, still a constant in my mind.

I rose to my knees, wiping my hands on my cotton dress as I leaned forward, inspecting a particularly vibrant bloom. I cradled the flower in my palm—careful not to damage it—running my fingers up the stalk, over the other petals, and landing finally on the silky texture inside. The silver orb in the middle sprinkled pollen on my fingers, the dust glowing with the same moonlit hue.

I put my other hand to my mouth, covering the small giggle that pushed past my lips. It was exquisite. Divine. It had been so long since I'd wanted to create, an eternity since I'd been inspired to make something new and haunting and beautiful. I looked down to Ballam, who sat in observation beside me.

"What do we think, boy? Did I do good?" He whined, nudging closer to me in response. I bent a lower blossom down for him to inspect, causing him to sneeze. The corner of the garden erupted in a silvery glow as the pollen drifted through the air. I fell back laughing, wiping my face free of the glowing pollen as the dust settled around us.

"Such a unique flower, Cailleach."

The voice startled me as I scrambled to my feet. Arne was just at the edge of the flowerbed, watching the blooms with a thoughtful look. He wore pristine white pants trimmed in gold to match his ornate vest. The moonlight reflected off of it, the glow of the cloth amplifying his ethereal form in a way that reminded me of the true extent of the power he harnessed.

"Arne," I replied as I wiped my hands on the front of my gown, suddenly aware of how plain it looked next to him. "I wasn't aware you were visiting the garden tonight."

He strode closer, his hands clasped behind his back as he inspected some of the nearby bushes. "I wasn't aware I needed your permission to visit. Is this a garden for the gods?" He spun on his heels, lowering his gaze to me. "Or for the Divine?"

I bowed my head, feeling suddenly small in his presence. "No, Arne, you're more than welcome to visit the garden at any time. You just startled me, that's all."

"Are these new, Cailli?" He hummed as he circled me, coming to the other side of the night- blooming plants. "You've outdone yourself. They really are something."

He took a blossom in his hand, plucking it with a singular, forceful motion. I winced at the movement, watching the light in the flower die out as it lost contact with its life source.

"Cailleach," I corrected him, moving forward to take the bloom from his grasp. He snatched my wrist with his free hand, holding me close to him as he crushed the flower and let the wilted petals fall to the ground.

"But is that not what Death calls you? Cailli?" He smirked down at me, tightening his hold. "I assumed it was available for the rest of us to use."

Ballam growled at my feet, sliding himself between me and Arne as I pulled out of his grasp. I rubbed my wrist where he'd held me, already knowing there'd be bruising. Arne looked down at the hound, sneering at the sight.

"I've asked Death the same that I ask of you," I replied, trying to keep my voice steady. Arne was known to have a temper, but I'd never seen him so bold as to lay hands on me before, and I didn't want him to see the fear he'd caused me. "My name is Cailleach or the Divine. I would never afford you the disrespect of calling you something you did not desire. I just ask for the same consideration."

"My apologies, Divine," he said as he mimicked a bow. He turned, walking through the garden rows in silent observation of all I had created here. I didn't like the feel of him in this sacred space, his eyes peering down on my work in that snarky sort of judgement, as if my power was nothing more than a fun little passtime.

"What are you doing here, Arne?" I took a step forward, itching to be rid of his presence amongst my plants, but Ballam cut in front of me to keep me back.

Arne's laugh crept through the rows of plants, slow and subtle but paralyzing all the same. "You've caused quite a predicament bringing that mutt of yours here."

"If Ballam is this much of an issue, just let me send him back to Death." Even as I said it, my heart broke at the idea. I didn't want to lose Ballam. He'd only been with me for a short time, but he'd worked his way into my heart. The idea of not having him beside me each day was almost too difficult to imagine.

Arne just chuckled at my suggestion, shaking his head. "You see, Divine. I would love if it were that simple. But that dog there"—he turned as he walked, pointing to Ballam, who was now growling heavily at him—"he knows too much, walked our halls and seen our way of life. He was sent by Death to spy on us. And I cannot let him return."

I stepped in front of Ballam. "You will not harm him, Arne."

Arne paused, stopping mid stride as he appraised, clearly shocked by my outspokenness. He watched me for a moment, a muscle in his jaw feathering.

"You see," he finally said. He walked over to a nearby bush, running his too-rough fingers over the blooms and damaging them. "I wasn't sure what to do at first. I'll be honest, I wasn't quite sure how to kill a depthhound, especially one so closely linked to Death himself." A wicked smile curved across his lips as he added, "That kind of power requires special care to ensure it stays gone."

"No." I fought to get Ballam behind me, but he refused to listen—trying with all his strength to situate himself between me and the threat at hand. "You *will not* touch him," I repeated, throwing as much power as I could behind my voice.

"Funnily enough," Arne continued on as if I hadn't even opened my mouth, "Lukus has been testing theories as of late, ways to defend ourselves against Death in the event that he ever...overstepped." A wicked gleam shone in Arne's eyes, mirrored in the cruel grin creeping across his lips. "Were you aware that weapons could be forged in magic? Bestowed with otherworldly power in order to take down beings with...certain affinities for staying alive?" His steps were slow, powerful, as he backed us into a corner of the hedges. I looked around desperately for anything I could use to fight him off, to overpower him just long enough to get past him and out of the garden.

"Now, I'm not going to lie. It's not a simple process." He slid his hands into the pockets "He will suffer. Quite a bit, I'm sure. But it's a sacrifice I'm willing to make to ensure the safety of our realm."

"No!" I screamed, the vines of the garden rattling with my words, even causing Arne to falter for a moment. He recovered quickly, on me in a heartbeat.

He grabbed my face with his hand, the sticky feel of his fingers against my cheeks making my skin crawl as I clawed to break free from his grasp. I heard Ballam behind me, a chorus of barks and growls growing distant as something dragged him away. In one swift motion Arne spun me and held my back to his chest, my face still firmly in his grip as he forced me to look ahead.

A whimper slipped out of me as my mind tried to make sense of what my eyes were seeing. Lukus emerged from the shadows of the garden entrance, some sort of silver chain in hand. Symbols etched into the metal glowed with power as Ballam thrashed against the bindings. Whatever this magic was, it was too strong for Ballam's own. I wailed as I watched the chain rip at his skin as he fought to break free.

"We are doing this *for* you, Divine," Arne whispered into my ear, his breath on my neck instantly turning my stomach.

"Get your fucking hands off me," I spat.

Arne tsked, shaking his head in disappointment. "See, he's already corrupting you, Cailli. You'll understand eventually. Even thank us, I'm sure." He nodded to Lukus who held the chain taut, despite Ballam thrashing around. Lukus pulled out a silver blade, the metal catching in the moonlight as he rose it in the air.

"Ballam!" My voice broke with the force I screamed his name, falling to my knees as I watched the blade sink into the depthhound's eye. Ballam wailed, my heart shattering into a million pieces as I watched in helpless despair. Lukus pulled the blade back again and brought it down on the other eye.

"A creation of my own design, Cailleach! You should be proud of what I've accomplished for us, the level of safety this brings us as rulers!" The amusement in Arne's voice was sickening as I watched Lukus raise the now bloodied blade in the moonlight. "A weapon woven with power, embedded with the strength of battle. A weapon worthy of a god."

Tears ran hot and heavy down my face. My fingers clung to the ground beneath my palms as I pulled up mounds of dirt, trying to to claw my way to him. Arne's grasp shifted as he wrapped an arm around my waist, pinning me in place.

"Lukus, please. Don't do this," I begged. Ballam howled in pain but didn't stop fighting to get back to me, the chains now covered in the sticky black of the depthhound's blood.

"Sorry, Cailleach," Lukus called out. "You left us no choice." He raised his blade a third time, striking Ballam's chest and ripping the blade through the length of his body. Thick black blood and entrails poured out of the hound, his howls falling to a barely audible whimper as his legs gave out beneath him. I watched in horror as the depthhound took his last breath. My friend. My protector.

"You see, Caillie, you made us realize our utter lack of protection here. You helped us see the need for an armory, a trove of weapons that we could wield if the need ever came to take down certain powerful beings." His breath was heavy in my ear, his words skittering along my skin. I dug my hands into the already broken earth. "When you bring something as dangerous as a Depthhound within our borders, what other option do we have? We must protect ourselves. We have duties to uphold, afterall."

I buried my fingers deeper, reaching out to the roots, the vines and plants of my garden—letting that rage flood my magic as I called for them to rise up. The ground burst open, gnarled roots coming to life as they reached out to the gods surrounding me.

"You will pay for this," I vowed, the words an omen in the night as they left my lips.

As if my promise summoned him, Death appeared in a mist of black swirls. He broke through the shadows like he'd been running between worlds, eyes wild as he took in the scene of Lukus towering over his depthhound and Arne pinning me beneath his grasp. He looked from Ballam to me, pain laced through his dark eyes.

Without a moment of hesitation, he was in front of Arne, whispering something above me as his shadows coiled around Arne's body. The shadows sunk into Arne's skin, igniting an uproar of panicked screams from the God of Power. He stumbled backwards as Death scooped my body into his arms and turned to face Lukus.

He was frozen, stunned at Death's apparition. Recognition set in and he took a step forward, blade swinging through the air— but Death was quicker.

Before Lukus's foot even touched the ground, the image of the garden dissolved around us and I knew we were once again traveling between realms. I tucked my head against Death's chest as I wailed, Ballam's cries still ringing in my ears. I didn't know how to put into words the pain that overtook my body. The betrayal I felt from the other deities and the shame I felt in Death's presence. He didn't turn me away though. We clung to one another as his magic swept us back into his realm. Back into the Depths.

CHAPTER 14
The Divine

The stillness of Death's chambers enveloped us. My face remained buried against his chest as he made his way over to the sofa. Tears streamed down my face, soaking his dark tunic as I balled my fists into the material. The pain in my chest only grew; no amount of crying, wailing, or deep breaths made it relent. But Death held me through it all, never urging me to move, never rushing me to settle.

Ballam hadn't even been mine. Not really. He belonged to Death. Yet here he was consoling me through this gut-wrenching loss. I sat up, swiping my face clear of the tears that wouldn't stop falling.

"Death, I am so sorry, I didn't know they would—"

"Shh, Cailli." He put his hands up, motioning for me to take a breath. "Why are you apologizing? This is not your fault. How could you have known they'd attack?" He was trying to stay calm for my sake, but I could see the pain swelling behind his eyes.

I buried my face in my hands, refusing to hold his stare as a new wave of grief washed over me. I refused to accept that I wasn't responsible for this in some way.

"I should have done more, should have fought harder." I shook my head frantically, replaying the series of events over in my mind. "I could have done *something*."

"You did," Death whispered as he reached forward, gently pulling my hands away from my face. He let them fall between us, cradling mine in his as he brushed his fingers rhythmically over my wrists. "I saw the garden come to life, goddess. I saw your power at work."

I grimaced, shaking my head again. "No, that wasn't enough. It didn't *do* anything."

"It did enough," he pushed back.

I met his eyes finally, tears welling in my eyes again, threatening to spill as the sounds of Ballam's cries continued ringing through my mind. I pulled my hand back from Death and clutched at my chest.

"What good is being a goddess when I feel so powerless?"

"Cailli, if you hadn't fought back—" His voice broke as he leaned in, stroking my damp cheek. "It would have been you I found gutted on the ground, not just Ballam."

"No," I whispered, unsure if the word had echoed just through my mind or also through the room around us. "They wouldn't. Would they?" My questioning, tear-filled eyes searched frantically for something to grab onto, settling finally on the grim reality reflected in his own eyes. He nodded silently, giving me time and space to process.

They were supposed to be my family. We ruled over the realms together, equals and friends. But had it ever truly felt like that? For deep down I must have always known. Even as I filled flowerbeds outside Estrid's window for her to gaze past them, as I excused Arne's trampling of the wildflowers for his over exuberant power, as I absorbed Lukus' snakelike words as the counsels of a true friend... As I looked back, I realized a part of me always knew I was never truly accepted. I'd lied to myself, convinced myself that there was a mutual respect there. That I was their equal. But nothing could have been further from the truth.

I swallowed hard, suppressing the urge to crumble completely. "Ballam should have been here, with you."

"Ballam has been my companion for quite some time." He pursed his lips together, looking off to the other side of the room as if recalling some distant memory. His muscles flexed, anger beneath the surface threatening to break through. "He was loyal and good, and he will be greatly missed. But—" He turned back to me, taking my hand once again in his. "He knew his job was to protect you. And I believe he succeeded. Till the very end." A beat of silence passed between us as Death sat back, folding his arms over his chest and rubbing at his chin.

Anger began boiling within me again, seeing Death mourn his companion. He was so stoic, so withheld in his emotions, but I could see the subtle shift in his features. There was sorrow in his eyes, a firm set to his jaw, as if he was trying to hold something back.

And it made me furious. They had no right, no reason to enact such viciousness. I was so tired of the violence, so tired of the pain and death and feeling so powerless. Something cracked in my mind, revealing centuries of trapped and hidden emotions: rage, pain, grief, weakness. They rose in me, one after another as my mind spiraled. It wasn't right. The power that they all were capable of, to take and kill and harm whatever and whoever they damn well pleased. Arne, Lukus, the fae that had attacked me. They were all the same—power-hungry males who would never stop, were too far gone for redemption of any kind. There had been a time not too long ago when the thought of harming another creature felt impossible. But now...

I stood, surprising Death as he looked up at me through eyes wide as the full moon.

"Take me to him," I ordered. My magic pulsed beneath my skin, igniting a fire I had not felt for so long. I'd spent my whole life being told what to do, who I was. No longer would I sit down and take this cruelty. It was time to right their wrongs. And I knew exactly where I needed to start.

Death cocked his head, trying to understand my meaning. Realization dawned on him though, and he slowly rose to his feet beside me.

"Cailli." His voice was low, a warning of the path I was about to embark on. I didn't care. I needed to do *something*. Ballam was gone. The deities who took his life were in another realm, a world away. I could do nothing to avenge him right now.

But there was something here that deserved my wrath.

The face that stared at me in watchful evaluation was the male I'd come to know—the kindhearted, somber being. He was letting me see the real version of him once more, not just the mask of Death but the male beneath.

"Are you sure?' He took my hand, his grasp gentle as he waited for me to decide.

"Yes," I answered at last. "I want to see him. Now." Before I lost my courage. Before my magic simmered and I talked myself out of what I was about to do.

That was all the answer he needed.

Death's shadows shrouded us in darkness, enveloping us whole and transporting us through the Depths. The sensation knocked the breath out of me and as I stuck a hand out to steady myself, I discovered we were no longer within the confines of his chambers.

My fingers grazed the stone walls of some deeper level of the Depths. The air was chilled, the walls and stone floor damp. A beaten up wooden door that resembled some sort of entrance to a dungeon lay just beyond. My head spun as I tried to piece myself back together. I clung desperately to my quickly collapsing courage. I breathed deeply, my eyes bouncing between him and the door. My stomach clenched as I knew what, or rather who, laid within.

"A peace offering," he said as he unlatched the door and pushed it open.

I looked from him to the dark chamber beyond, letting my eyes adjust to the light within. I took a tentative step inside, the rage that fueled me suddenly dispersing. A crumpled form sat in the middle of the room, chained to the wall behind as another dark form stood off to the side. I recognized the creature to the side from that night in the mortal realm—one of Death's Daeomis. But the being in the middle of the chamber was coated in blood, both dried and fresh. Their face was swollen from what I assumed were several rounds of beatings, to the point that their features were unrecognizable. But as they raised their head to speak, a sinister, raspy laugh croaked out of a too swollen mouth.

The same laugh that haunted my nightmares every night since I was attacked in the mortal realm.

"Hello again, darling."

I backed out of the room, turning down the hallway and leaning against the cool stone wall. "I can't," I said over and over again. Death was beside me in an instant, bending over to stare up at me from where I leaned.

"Cailli, you can. Trust me."

"I don't know what I was thinking. This was a mistake, Death. My magic doesn't work that way."

"Yet," Death added, lifting me by the shoulders so I stood to face him.

"No, not yet. It just *doesn't*. You think if I could have done something to stop Lukus and Arne from killing Ballam I wouldn't have done it? I tried!" I shook my head, squeezing my eyes closed. "I thought I could but I *can't*," I repeated, pacing the corridor as I tried to calm my reeling mind. Conflicting emotions crashed over me, my desire to release the pain and grief and anger still building inside me at odds with my belief of who I was, what I was capable of.

"I saw you, goddess. I saw that wrath inside you bring that garden to life. You *can*, Cailleach. You just need some guidance."

I paused my pacing, picturing the vines that had reached for Arne and Lukus. *My* vines, doing *my* bidding. I pushed the idea out before it could even take root.

"No, that was... I don't know what that was. Even if I could get my power to manifest in that way—" I turned back to the room where the fae sat in his own filth. "That is my creation, Death. My responsibility. It's not the same for me as it is for you. I made a mistake asking you to bring me down here."

Death rested his hands on my shoulders, turning me away from the entrance of the cell to face him. "He may be your creation, goddess. But he doesn't deserve life. You don't know his list of atrocities, but I do." Death's jaw hardened as he narrowed his gaze on me. "You were not the first he attacked, Cailleach. And the others..." He looked off to the side, swallowing hard as he tamped down on the power I could see filling the small space around us. "Let's just say the others didn't get to walk away. Is your duty not also to them? Are you not also responsible for maintaining that creation?"

My eyes stung with unshed tears as I forced air into my lungs. He was right, I knew he was right. It's why I'd even asked him to bring me here in the first place. But now that I was here, now that I could see him, sense his presence and his soul... I didn't have the strength to be the one to claim it. I looked down at my hands, pure and untainted with the stain of death.

"Violence is not always the answer, Death." My voice cracked as I spoke, trying to convince myself as much as I was him.

He moved his hands up the curve of my neck, grabbing my face and pulling my attention back to him.

"Sometimes, goddess, it is."

I blinked as a single tear fell down my face. He wiped it away with a simple stroke of his thumb, holding my gaze for a long time. I nodded finally, swallowing the fear I felt inside me. He mirrored the motion, nodding with me as he guided me back to the doorway.

"I'll be right beside you. I'll guide you the whole way if you need me to."

He took my hand in his and we stepped into the dimly lit cell together, two cosmic forces clashing together to find the balance we both desperately needed.

The chained fae sneered as we entered, no doubt sensing the fear and trepidation coming from me. Death let a shadow slip out, pulling at the chains binding his hands behind his back. He fell backwards, landing hard on his shoulder with a sickening crunch.

"Do you remember what you did in the garden to call forth that kind of power?"

I grimaced at his question, picturing Ballam in all that pain. I had to feel it, though. I knew leaning into that grief and rage would only serve to push me further within the well of my power.

After several painful moments, I closed my eyes and nodded. My rage was right at the surface, so ready to be tapped. Death stepped out of the way, keeping his hand in mine as he whispered beside me:

"Now focus, goddess. Think about everything this monster did to you." He gave me a moment, feeling the rage deepen as I recalled the memory of another horrendous night. Through my closed eyelids I could still feel my skin beginning to glow a deep golden as I raised my arm, letting my magic flow.

"Good girl," Death praised. Something about the way he said it had my core tightening.

"Now think about turning that rage on him, Cailli. Make him pay for what he did." I took a deep breath, doing just as he instructed me to do. He leaned in, his breath warming my ear as he whispered, "Make it hurt."

A moment passed in silence, then another. I concentrated, letting Death's instructions radiate through my mind, my body. The fae before us taunted me, calling out insults and fueling my rage.

A sound crept into the cell, a sort of slithering echoed only by the cracking of stone. A smile broke across my face as I looked up at the ceiling, watching as roots from the world above drove into the Depths. They broke through the barrier between worlds, snaking into the chamber and down the walls of the small cell.

I dropped my gaze to the fae on his knees before me, watching for the exact moment his face fell in terror.

"Oh shi—" The curse never left his lips as the roots shot through him, bursting forward and wrapping around his face, his chest, ripping him apart. The room exploded, showered in a hot, red rain.

I marveled in the sight, surprising myself at the feeling of pure, unadulterated pride and power as the golden glow of my skin filled the small cell. Death had been right. About me, about my power. He'd seen something within me that no one else had, and now I stood here, fully encompassed in my newfound power. Yet, something about it felt so familiar, as if I was returning home rather than discovering something new within me.

I turned to Death, overcome with emotion. He stepped before me, his shadows wrapping around us. Their dark presence trickled over my skin, no doubt checking to see if I was okay. I didn't know how to thank him, how to explain to him everything that was running through my mind. Nothing felt good enough, nothing could ever portray how grateful I was for him helping me feel this power.

Lost in a haze of pride and drunk off my own power, I threw myself forward. My lips crashed against his, hungry and desperate.

CHAPTER 15
Death

Cailli pulled away, entirely too soon for my liking. I hadn't expected her to react like that, somehow discovering the true extent of her power unlocking those deep, inherent longings. But now that she'd shown those pieces of herself, I couldn't stop myself.

"I'm sorry, I don't know why—"

I was on her in a second, hands pressed to her cheeks, leaving ruby streaks against her skin. My lips found hers without hesitation, my shadows dancing around us, ready to claim her as my own. My beautiful, wonderful, goddess—painted in the blood of her enemies. I'd have her no other way.

Her muscles tensed as my tongue chased hers, but within a blink of an eye her body was melting into mine. She wrapped her arms around me, letting me consume her. My shadows grew, enveloping us in an obsidian mist. When she finally broke away, gasping for air, she shrieked to find us back in my chambers high above the filth of the dungeon.

"How do you keep doing that?" she asked, breath raspy as she tried to recover.

"For how long will you forget that I am ruler of this realm? I have many tricks up my sleeve," I laughed as I moved in again, locking my lips on hers with a violent sort of hunger. I guided her down the hall to my main bathing chamber, never taking my mouth off hers. I clicked the door shut, pushing her up against it as I finally broke away from her mouth only long enough to find the curve of her neck that never failed to catch my eye when she was around. I breathed in her scent, my eyes rolling as I craved more of her.

"Do you want this, goddess?" I asked, hovering above her skin as I waited for her reply.

"Do I—what?" she asked, stunned and breathless. Even as she processed the words, her body pushed into mine, begging for more.

I ground my teeth, willing every last semblance of restraint into my body. "Do. You. Want. This." I repeated my question through clenched teeth, watching the steady rise and fall of her chest. "Tell me now if you want me to stop, because even one moment longer with you like this and I won't be able to hold back."

I watched the bob of her throat as she swallowed. I couldn't force myself to pry my eyes off that porcelain skin now stained with red, couldn't keep the power thrumming in my mind at bay, to do anything but focus on the hollow of her collar bone as I waited for her reply.

"Yes, Death," she finally responded, her voice sounding more sure, more powerful, than I'd ever heard it before. "Yes, I want this. I want you."

"In all the Depths," I growled, mesmerized, before burying my head in her neck, licking and sucking and biting until I tasted that beautiful tang of iron. She squealed but didn't pull away as I licked the small bead of blood from her neck. It tasted as good as I knew it would, pure and full of her golden light. The taste of her power laced through her blood was addicting, consuming, and I would live every day for the rest of eternity chasing that high.

I pulled away, finally looking her in the eyes as her labored breaths filled the room with the scent of her desire.

"Hmm," I purred. "What a filthy little goddess." She looked down at her dress, covered in a mixture of soil, blood, and sweat. The sight of it had her retreating from the space we shared, slipping back into the world beyond this moment. I snagged her chin with my finger, forcing her eyes back to mine. "Let me clean you."

She nodded, raising her hands above her head as I guided the sullied dress off her body. I discarded the clothing, taking her hand in mine as I backed into the bathing chamber. I reached into the bathing stall, turning the knob to let the water flow. Cailli looked up in awe as thousands of streams of water fell from the tap above. The chamber quickly filled with steam from the heated water, bringing a rosy tint to her skin.

I kept my eyes dutifully trained on her face, knowing that if I allowed my gaze to dip lower, there would be no patience for time to clean up.

"What in the stars is this?" she asked as she stuck her hand into the rain, letting the warmth of the water draw her in. "How?"

She turned around to me, the water splashing off her back as she hesitated to submerge herself fully.

"Hot springs," I answered, letting my lips turn up at the look of wonderment on her face. "We discovered a system of hot springs within the caverns above. Tapped into it to create these." She broke her gaze away from where the water fell from the ceiling, snapping her attention back to me.

"There's more of them?" she asked, amazed. I couldn't help but chuckle.

"Goddess, there's so much more. And I plan to show you all of it." I lifted the bloodstained tunic over my head, dropping it by my feet, and unfastened my pants as I stepped towards the rainfall. Cailli's eyes traced the muscles on my chest, her gaze falling lower as I let my pants fall, kicking them to the side. Her mouth popped open in silent appreciation as I stepped into the bathing stall, forcing her back into the stream of water.

She gasped, the noise going straight to my cock as I watched her back arch at the sudden heat. There was so much I wanted to do to her, so much I wanted to show her and let her discover in her own time. My mind was at war with my body. I reached out, tipping her head back to let the water soak her long copper hair. It ran down her naked body, swirling with the splatter of blood and dirt—washing the filth away as I let my hands trace its tracks.

She never hesitated, never flinched as she let me run my hands down the length of her. She just watched me through those golden, glowing eyes, dripping with desire. Her power still pounded through her body; I could feel it just beneath her skin as I let my fingers explore. It only pushed me further, deepening my need to have her.

"Sit," I ordered, pointing to the cutout in the stone behind me. Her desire turned to curiosity, but she didn't argue as she stepped past me, sinking into the makeshift seat carved into the stone. I let the water pelt into my back as I licked my lips, enjoying the view of her sitting so compliantly as she obeyed my command.

Then I sunk to my knees, trying not to smirk as her eyes went wide.

"Cailleach, the Divine. *My* goddess," I called out, taking her hand in mine and planting a kiss against her upturned palm. "From this day forward, I vow to protect, to obey"—I hooked my hand behind her knee, placing another kiss to the inside of her leg—"and to worship"—I mirrored my kiss on the other leg, looking back up to her from my position, kneeling before her—"only you."

The air thinned as she looked at me, any note of playfulness gone. "Death," she whispered, shocked by my proclamation.

"I have needed you for so long, Cailli. Never could I have imagined you returning that desire. I have watched you questioning your worth and your strength for centuries—the whole time, dying inside not being able to show you what I saw. I will not waste another day doing so."

Water droplets mixed with the tears that trailed down her face. She tried to blink them away, but seeing her beautiful and broken was a sight to behold. I relished it, just as I did with every moment I spent in her presence.

"It starts now, Cailli," I promised. My lips tipped up with wicked need as I leaned into her, pressing my body between her legs. "And it starts with this." I sunk myself between her, letting my lips taste every part of her as she met me.

"Death," she panted, letting her hand fall to my hair and find purchase there. I growled in approval as she fisted my dark strands, entwining her fingers and pulling me closer. I sucked tenderly, nipping at her sensitive bud. She cried out, her back arching towards me as I took the opportunity to slip my fingers inside her.

She groaned in approval, her other hand flying up behind her to grab anywhere she could on the stone wall. Her breathing turned ragged, her cries louder as I took more of her. The bathing stall filled with my shadows, growing deeper in response to her climb. I let one slip out from the mist, snaking its way up her body and clamping down on the peak of her breast.

"Death!" She cried out in pure ecstasy.

I grinned in delight as she came with my name on her lips. Pumping my fingers a few more times, I ran my tongue over her to drag out her pleasure.

"That was…" Her words were breathy, distant, as I released her, pulling both of us to our feet and wrapping my arms around her. I let my lips crash against hers once more, letting the taste of her fresh on my tongue roll through her mouth. I wanted her to feel her magic, taste it, and see for herself how powerful it was. I vowed to make sure she would never doubt her power again.

CHAPTER 16
Karmi

I chewed nervously on my bottom lip as I waited in our chambers for my sister to return. My eyes were glued to the entryway, my ears straining for the smallest sound to hint that Sophia had made it back to our realm safely. I could feel my lip turn raw, the iron tang on my tongue serving as a warning to stop with my fidgeting. I couldn't, though. Not until I knew how things had gone in the mortal realm.

Theora poured herself a cup of tea beside me. She was the picture of poised serenity—as always.

"Honestly, Karmi, you need to calm down," she chided as she set the teapot back on the low table before us. "There's no use worrying so, we will know soon enough."

I pried my eyes away from the double doors, taking in the measure of her composure.

"How can you be so calm about this, sister?"

She was never one to lose control—but I couldn't imagine a more fitting time to let nerves take hold. My knuckles went white as I clutched onto the fabric of my skirts in my lap, turning my attention back to the doors.

"It is not a matter of *if* we will succeed, but *when*," Theora answered over the clinking of the spoon stirring honey into her tea. Two scoops to be exact, in the same floral black tea blend that had become her favorite as of late. Before it had always been the sickly sweet blend of fruity herbal tea the deities loved—a mix of rose and other florals along with dried fruit like raspberries, cherries, and pomegranate. None of us preferred it, but stocking anything else had become challenging with the eyes of the deities constantly on us, constantly limiting the resources available to us *lesser* beings. How Theora had been able to secure such a stock of the black tea was beyond me, but I was thankful for the reprieve in our private chambers as I poured myself a cup.

Theora was many things, but impulsive was not one of them. I knew she'd been planning this for a long time, longer than she'd let on with either me or Sophia when she'd finally shared the full scale of her hopes. After the fall out with the Divine's journey to the Depths, and after her discovery of the missing tome from our archives—hidden carefully within Lukus' chambers—Theora had an idea. She'd been digging, looking at the records of each deity: the full scale of their recorded power, the origin of that power, and the true extent of their duties in the realms. She wouldn't explain it fully, but apparently she'd come across some useful information—something that could prove *how* the other deities had been deceitful about the relationship between Death and the Divine. I pushed for more details, but all she would share is that this could help us restore order amongst the realms.

I was okay with not understanding fully. I trusted her more than I trusted myself most days. She had always taken care of us for centuries and there was no doubt in my mind that she would continue to do so, no matter what.

But the stakes now were so high—the risks, so much more terrifying than anything we'd faced before. If we could alert the Divine without drawing the others' attention, if we could get her to believe and accept her rightful place above them, then perhaps we could repair the realms. The violence would stop, the abuse at the hands of the other deities. I was desperate for that, desperate for our plan to work. That desperation is what had led me to give Death the missing tome—rather than hiding it in the mortal realm as Theora had instructed me to do—in hopes he'd figure out a way to get through to the Divine.

Guiding her to this without catching the other deities' attention would be near impossible, especially now. When she had challenged them, brought a piece of Death within this realm... the fate of that poor animal was too cruel. Visions of my own fate ending beneath their blade haunted me every night since I took record of their actions.

"I know you believe in our success, sister. And I trust you—really, I do." Theora scowled at me over the rim of her teacup, sensing where this conversation was going. It was no secret to her that I held a bit of trepidation for the path she was leading us down. "But what happens if they find out, if we get caugh—"

"Enough, Karmi." Her tone was curt, her words short and irritable as she leaned over, grabbing onto my arm. "You keep speaking doubt into this scheme and you may as well send us to the Depths yourself." Her gaze narrowed on me, her words pressing into me with a fierce severity. I gulped down, trying to slow my racing heart as I made myself meet her stare. I nodded frantically, trying with every fiber of my being to push out the fears and doubts still ravaging my mind.

I opened my mouth to speak, unsure what I was even preparing to say, when a hurried set of footsteps echoed down the corridor. Both our heads whipped up to the doorway as we watched Sophia slip into our chambers. My breath caught in my throat as I searched her body for any signs of injury, any clue as to the events of the night. I knew Theora's eyes were on her too, waiting with bated breath to hear confirmation of her hopes for the evening.

Sophia looked from me to Theora and back, her face drained of all color, her breath ragged and shallow as she pressed herself against the door—as if to keep out whatever was on the other side. She made no sound, but the light fell from her eyes as she held our gaze and shook her head slowly.

I rushed to her side within an instant, taking her arm and leading her over to the sofa. "There were no signs of her?" I pushed, desperate for more details. "What did you see?"

"Karmi." Theora cut me a stern warning to back off as Sophia collapsed against the plush cream cushions.

"I'm so sorry, Theora." Sophia buried her face in her hands. "I searched every inch of the realms we can access. I even tried to sneak into the Depths, but it was no use. Death has her and isn't letting anyone get close."

"Perhaps this is for the best, perhaps this will afford the Divine the opportunity to learn the truth," I reasoned.

Theora closed her eyes, steadying her breath as she ignored me and recentered herself. "It's okay, Sophia. At least we know she's protected—for now." She opened her eyes once more and tenderly reached forward, taking Sophia's hands in her own and urging them away from her face.

"And what of my other request?" Theora asked, stooping to catch Sophia's gaze. Defeat gave way to excitement, her eyes shimmering with something secretive and mischievous.

"That," she answered, producing a folded piece of parchment from the pocket of her skirts, "was much more manageable."

Sophia unfolded the parchment slowly, careful not to tear the fragile paper. I leaned over the writing, trying to make sense of it in the darkness of our chambers. Theora shooed me away, plucking the paper out of Sophia's hands and bringing it closer to the firelight. Her brow pinched together in concentration as she read over the ancient writing. Before long, a slow smile crept across her lips.

"You've done well, Sophia," she called out at last, folding the parchment and tucking it inside her own pocket.

"What does that mean?" I asked as Theora paced by the hearth. I looked between my two sisters, lost to shock as I waited for one of them to make sense of this. I hadn't been aware of a second task. I thought her purpose was to scout the mortal realms, in search of any sign of the Divine or any possible passage into the Depths.

"It means…" Theora slowed her pacing to face us. "That we were right. It means that our years of abuse and degradation are finally coming to an end. And it will be all the easier to achieve with the help of this parchment."

She stalked over to the sofa, holding out a hand each for me and my sister. We took her open palms, forming a makeshift circle as our oldest sister towered over us. I stared into those dark blue, hardened eyes—the same shade as Sophia's, yet somehow colder. I caught sight of my own reflection in the mirror hanging above the hearth behind her. Contrasting pools of blue-green stared back at me.

Theora and I were opposites in so many ways. She was often cold, determined—the leader of the three of us. She took the brunt of the abuse from the deities, the majority of the more labor-intensive responsibilities, and she always took the fall for us when need be. But her caring nature ended there. So I became the sister who could listen, who could be a reminder that the world needn't always be so serious, so scary. Sophia was a simple mixture of the both of us, but more than anything she was known for her sweet disposition and her calming sense of peace. I think our biggest concern in this life was to protect her from the deities, to preserve that sweet innocence, because we knew the world would need it one day.

"The time has come for them to understand the weight of their actions," Theora said. I could see the determination in her face as she looked down on us with pride and excitement, but there was something else in her deep blue eyes. Something dangerous and reckless. Something so unlike a scribe, and it frightened me. "It means we have everything we need to follow through with our plans. To restore order and to right the wrongs that have gone on for far too long."

She raised her head, staring off into some unseen timeline. Always assessing, always checking to make sure our path was clear.

"It is time for their deception to be unearthed. Time for the true rulers to take their place."

CHAPTER 17
The Divine

Death guided me out of the hot springs, after making sure any trace of blood and dirt was gone from my body. He produced a few towels from a nearby cabinet and worked to dry my skin, my hair. His touch was gentle as he trailed the towel over me. His tenderness was striking, so different from how I'd expected him to be. And it only made me want him more.

He discarded the towels, replacing them with long, silken dressing robes. He led me out the door and down the hall, entering a much larger chamber dripping with elegance and status. I gaped, taking in the extravagant sight.

Velvet, oversized sofas were positioned around a sunken sitting room, arranged to face a massive black hearth. The midnight stone extended all the way to the ceiling of the chamber, practically sparkling when it caught the light. Off to the other side stood a massive bed draped in more silk bedding. An ornate wooden headboard framed the bed, embellished with ancient and hauntingly beautiful carvings. The rich, brown hues of the wooden furniture melded against the blacks and deep greens of the velvet and leather sofas, all dripping with the warm splash of candlelight from the hundreds of lit candles hanging on the chandelier high above, and from the many candelabras scattered throughout the vast room. It was a chamber fit for a god.

I could not hide my absolute amazement, my mouth falling wide open.

"What, you didn't think the Ruler of the Underworld lived in that tiny room, did you?" A satisfied kind of amusement settled over him as he looked back at me with a twinkle in his eye.

Anticipation swirled low in my belly, heating and traveling lower still. I didn't know how it had come to this. We'd been at odds with each other for as long as I could remember. But if what Death said was true, perhaps that wasn't totally honest. Perhaps there was a fine line between love and hate, contempt and desire—between loathing and lovers.

Death gestured for me to sit, dropping my hand and striding over to an inset counter next to the obsidian hearth. I settled into one of the sofas, running my hand slowly across the dark green velvet and relishing in its feel. I tucked my legs under me, propping my elbow against the low back of the sofa and watched as Death filled two glasses with something from a decanter.

He turned, a glass in each hand, and made his way back over to me. A smug look settled across his face as he handed me my drink.

"What?" I asked, pretending like I wasn't just ogling at the sight of him.

He hummed, taking a long pull from his glass—refusing to take his eyes off me. His teeth clicked together as he swallowed another sip of whatever spirits he'd poured for us.

"Did you enjoy the hot springs?" He set his drink down on an end table, perching on the edge of the sofa.

"Hmm?" I repeated, not quite paying attention, only thinking of the feel of his lips still igniting my skin.

He gestured back down the hall to the bathing chamber. "The hot springs."

"Ah," I replied, incapable of focusing on anything besides how desperately I wanted to feel his touch again. "Yes, it was quite...pleasant."

"Cailli," he purred as he moved closer, taking my hand in his. "There's so much I want to show you, teach you. But I want to be sure that you want this too."

"I already told you," I started to argue, but he cut me off.

"You told me you want me. And as relieved as I am to hear that, it's not what I'm asking now."

I waited for him to explain as he closed his eyes and squeezed my hand a little tighter.

"You are so good. So pure, goddess. And as much as I love that about you..." He paused, scrubbing a hand through his still wet sable hair. "As much as I love that, I need you to know how badly I want to change it, too."

My brows furrowed as I looked away, taking a sip from my glass. The spirits burned the back of my throat as I swallowed. I was thankful for the sensation, pulling me back to the present out of the blissful fog that had settled over my mind.

"What does that mean?" I finally asked, fidgeting nervously with the glass in my hand.

"It means that you and I are opposite. In every way possible. I am darkness and you are light. And as much as I love seeing your light, I'd be lying if I said I didn't want to taint it with some of my own darkness." He huffed out a breath, rolling his neck as he suddenly stood from the sofa. "I'm failing miserably at explaining this." He sighed before downing the rest of his drink and moving to refill it.

"I think," he finally said as he strode back towards me, "that we can offer each other a sort of balance that we haven't had before. When you're with me, you don't *have* to be just light, just creation." He swooped in on me, lust heavy in his dark black eyes. "Seeing you today—seeing you harness that power and take that life... It did things to me, Cailli. Darkness looked so beautiful on you, I can't help but wonder what your light could do to me."

His gaze pored over me, desperate, searching. I clung to my glass, my knuckles going white with nerves under the weight of his affection. But I met his gaze, letting his pride reach my own. I knew I should feel guilt for what I'd done. I wanted to. But even now as the heat of that moment had worn off, I felt nothing for that vile creature that had attacked me, nothing but pride in the vicious power that had manifested inside me. And I knew Death understood that feeling well.

"But it also brought forth that darkness in me," Death continued, pulling my attention back to his frenzied state. "It called out for you. Not to claim your life, but your *soul*. I told you that I needed you, goddess. Not want, *need*. And right now I need to know how much of my darkness you can take."

I gulped down the rest of my drink, handing him the empty glass—a silent demand for more. He smirked, taking the glass and refilling it quickly before perching again on the edge of the sofa. I took the glass and drank deeply, trying to find courage to give him the answer already circling in my mind.

I swallowed down the last mouthful of the drink and reached around Death, setting the glass down on the end table behind him, using the excuse to close the space between us. I raised to my knees to reach his face. Wrapping my hand around the back of his neck, I pulled him in till we were nose to nose.

Here before me was a male so different than I would have ever expected. We'd spent our existences in misunderstanding, fearing the other sides of ourselves we saw reflected in one another. And then he saved me, showed up for me when no one else had, and pushed me to discover that strength inside me that the others had tried to dismiss. I'd spent my life feeling weak, yet he saw my strength and helped me discover it for myself. I was quickly coming to realize... he was my everything.

"Death," I exhaled, letting the smoky aroma of the spirits surround us. "I want you. On your darkest day and on your lightest. I will give you my light when your darkness feels heavy and I will take your shadows whenever you're willing to give them. I knew what I was signing up for when you led me into those hot springs." I moved even closer, letting my lips drift dangerously close to his as I added, " And I still said yes." I sealed my vow with a kiss, letting my lips dance across his with every ounce of intent and hope I had for our future.

He broke away, letting out a sigh of relief as he rested his forehead against mine.

"This moment right here has made every century of waiting worth it."

I stifled a laugh, reaching up and planting another kiss on his lips before settling back down on my knees. "So what's next?" I asked, my lips curling up in anticipation.

Death's eyes fixated on me as he set his still full glass on the table behind him. "Next, goddess...I show you my world." He rose to his feet, taking my hand and leading me over to the bed in the far corner. "Lie down," he instructed. I did as he said, scooting back against the silk.

Death sucked his lower lip between his teeth and I couldn't help but think about the feel of my skin between them. My hand fluttered over the bite mark he'd left on my neck.

"What's on your mind, Cailli?" His eyes were still filled with lust, but I could hear the concern in his voice as he watched my movements.

"You keep flashing those teeth as if you don't know what it does to me." I barely recognized my own voice—so confident, so filled with desire. The concern melted away, replaced only by primal need as Death loomed over me.

"Hands up. Now."

I threw him an inquisitive look but obeyed, letting my hands fall back above my head. The movement caused my gown to fall open, exposing me fully to him. I suppressed the urge to wince, trying to cling to the confidence I'd felt moments earlier. He slipped his own dressing gown off, painfully slow, as he left me waiting and wanting. He walked around the bed, shadows trailing in his wake. I turned my head to keep him in my sight, to get a better view of his body fully on display for me. I jumped as the icy feeling of his power crept over my skin.

"Death…" I called out, hesitant to give into the shadows suddenly snaking across me.

"Trust me, goddess." He stopped by the foot of the bed, so distant from me. He crossed his arms and watched as he directed his shadows up my arms and over my wrists, binding them in place. The chill was bone deep, but I didn't shrink away from it. They felt like cool spring water, trickling over my skin in a cruel, salacious taunt. Gooseflesh broke out across my body, the peaks of my breasts pebbling instantly.

The shadows didn't stop there but rather trailed down, wrapping around my neck, sliding down my stomach, and sinking into the apex of my thighs. I gasped at the sensation, the chill of his shadows mixing with the heat of my desire.

"Focus, Calli. Are you listening?"

My eyes shot open, unaware that I'd even closed them as I sunk into the feel of his shadows tightening against me. I nodded my head, so full with need that I found it hard to form words.

"Answer, Cailli. Out loud."

"Yes," I breathed. Death rewarded me with several strokes from the shadow pressing against my core. I cried out, throwing him an incredulous look when the motion stopped.

"Good girl," he hummed. "I need you to make me a promise, goddess. If things go too far and you no longer feel safe, I need you to promise that you will use that beautiful voice of yours to tell me to stop."

My brows furrowed in irritation. "I already told you—"

"It doesn't matter what you said. I need it to be clear that you will always have a say, even if you change your mind. Now, don't make me ask again."

The shadows around my wrists tightened. A curve of a smile danced across my lips as I debated pushing him further. But as he stood there, arms crossed with a stone-cold look upon his face, I knew he was serious. And no matter how hard I tried to convince him that I wanted all of him, every dark desire, he wouldn't touch me until he knew I had a safe way out.

He edged onto the bed, leaning over me with a severe expression. Gone was the lighthearted male who'd just poured his heart out to me moments ago, who'd gotten on his knees before me and vowed to worship me for all eternity. This was the face of Death, and I couldn't take my eyes off him as he inched closer to me.

"Promise me." It wasn't a question, nor a request. It was an ultimatum. Even now in this close proximity, he didn't touch me. Wouldn't touch me. Not until he knew I took this as seriously as he did. My face fell, finally understanding the weight of this decision for him. I nodded swiftly, reaching out desperately to find my voice.

"Okay, Death. I promise."

Those four words were Death's undoing.

He tried to hide it, but I didn't miss the subtle changes in his expression—the way his eyes widened just slightly, the muscles that tightened across his chest, his arms, as he tried to restrain himself. He was as desperate as I was and the thought had me smirking up at him, too smug for my own good.

He leveled a challenging look at me as he raised his hand over me, restricting the shadows and sending a new wave of that soul-shattering chill through me. His body lowered over me, even as his magic continued to stroke me—building a frantic need that took over my body. I wanted him on me, in me. I wanted it more than I had ever desired anything before. And I could tell my desperation was only encouraging him to move slower.

A wicked smile curled across his lips as he paused, watching me writhing beneath him. "I like seeing you wrapped in my shadows, goddess. It might be the most beautiful thing I've ever beheld."

"Death, please. Touch me," I cried out. Every time I felt my body starting to tip over the edge, he'd slow the steady rhythm of that taunting little shadow.

"Now where's the fun in that? I'm quite enjoying the view." His smirk deepened as I groaned at the new rhythm against my center.

"I need you," I begged. My wrists strained against the shadow holding them in place above my head, desperate to have my hands on him.

"You don't," Death refuted. "Not yet." He leaned forward, trailing his tongue over the path of his shadow down my stomach. I pushed up to him, encouraging him to dip lower, but he only laughed against my skin—stopping just shy of where I needed him. I let out a frustrated groan, letting my hips fall back to the bed.

Death grabbed hold of the shadow binding my wrists, pulling me up to him with a sudden force that had me shrieking. He sat back on his heels, tugging the shadow to let me fall against him. He ran his face over my cheek, down my neck and to that spot still sore from where he'd bit me earlier. The sensation went straight to my core, and I melted against him—unable to hold myself up.

"Come on, goddess. Convince me. Use that beautiful body to show me just how badly you want me."

I leaned into his touch, searching for his lips. Just as I'd achieved my goal and parted to let his tongue slip through, he threw me back down on the bed. Irritation flooded me, mixing with the heat that refused to let up no matter how many times he slowed his shadows.

My eyes rolled back into my head, letting the mixture of sensations take over me. I was utterly lost to the pleasure and pain coursing through my blood. My muscles restricted against his shadows, my body taking on a mind of its own as I again pushed closer to him in a desperate attempt to feel his touch. Not his shadows, not his magic—-but his hands, his mouth, his cock.

I heard him huff out a satisfied breath. I opened my eyes, gasping to find his skin cast in a vibrant golden glow. I followed the rays of light to realize it was my skin, my magic, coming to life and pushing back against his shadows.

"There it is," he breathed as his shadows rose from my body to twine around the rays of my light. The restraints lifted as our magic danced through the air, enveloping us in a shroud of darkness and light. The world beyond no longer existed. It was just me and Death in this sacred space, the collision of our power creating our own personal realm to exist in.

It was like removing a barrier, the pleasure ravaging my body increasing tenfold without the restraint of my power holding it back. I watched the beauty of our magic swirling together, so distracted that I squealed when Death grabbed me by the hips and sunk himself into me in one swift motion.

"So ready for me, aren't you, goddess?" His head lobbed back as he spoke. I ground my hips against him, begging for the friction. He only laughed through gritted teeth, head raised up to the ceiling as he tightened his grip on my hips to hold me in place.

"Don't tell me you can't handle more, Death," I teased between breathy groans, knowing the comment would earn me some sort of reaction. Death's head snapped back up, his eyes darkening as he looked down at me. He didn't say anything for a moment, just let his power build around us as if to show off just who was in control.

Finally, a shadow slipped out of the mist, snaking up my body and wrapping around my neck once more. "Remember your promise to me, goddess?" he asked, straining to hold himself back. I nodded, swallowing hard and feeling the shadow constrict against the motion.

"Good," he answered. "Don't break it." His words were heavy, haunting, laced with a hunger I couldn't wait to experience.

I met his gaze, making sure he could see the utter lack of hesitation in my eyes as I responded almost instantly: "Yes, sir."

Darkness erupted around us. Death slammed into me. His movements were vicious, violent—any shred of restraint completely obliterated as his power took over. He came to life before me, the full extent of his darkness filling the rest of the room. But it never snuffed out my light. His shadow tightened around my throat, ripping a scream of pleasure from my lungs. Tears stung at my eyes under the pressure, but I wanted more. I let my hips meet him with each stride, grabbing onto his knees to bury him deeper inside of me.

He roared, his voice booming through the room and stilling the pulsing power all around us. The sheer sound of him had me coming, crashing over the edge I'd been clinging to and free-falling into wild delirium as he chased me, falling forward and burying his face against me.

I panted, my body utterly exhausted from the drawn out pleasure, but my heart so full. I laced my hands through Death's hair, combing the silky strands and planting soft kisses against his forehead.

"I want this forever, Cailli. Want *you* forever. In this lifetime and the next. I will never stop wanting you."

His whispered proclamation stilled my fingers. The mist of magic around us slowly drifted away and brought us back to the room around us. He raised onto his elbow, tucking a piece of my hair behind my ear. "I mean it," he added. "I've been in love with you for so long. And I need you to know that, no matter how wild it sounds."

I looked into his eyes for what felt like an eternity, thinking over all the times we'd interacted. There had always been something there, a tension I never fully understood. We'd been taught to hate each other, conditioned to believe we couldn't possibly coexist. But as I looked up at him now, I realized he might in fact be the best thing that had ever happened to me, the missing piece I'd spent my life searching for. And the thought of losing him, of spending another day without him, terrified me to my core. Now that I knew what I could have, what I could be with him?

"I love you too, Death," I said softly, making a silent promise to myself that I would never go back.

CHAPTER 18
The Divine

I'd fallen asleep in that bliss, entangled in his arms and at peace for what felt like the first time in forever. But when I awoke, he was gone. I sat up, a frown settling across my lips as I let my eyes scan the room for him. A gentle click of the door snagged my attention as he walked into the chambers with two steaming teacups and a book tucked under his arm. He stopped by the table, dropping the tome on the surface. Relief flooded me as he strode over to the bed, offering me a cup. I thanked him, sipping deeply and relishing in its warm comfort.

After I'd drunk half the cup, I realized Death was already bathed and dressed. I eyed his pristine black clothing as he sipped his tea.

"I had some business to attend to this morning." He answered my unspoken question, catching the way my eyes lingered on him. "Which brings me to my next point." He grabbed the cup from my hands, and I reluctantly let it go. "I have something to show you."

He set both teacups on the bedside table, leading me out of the bed and down the hall. Excitement radiated off him as he opened the door to the bathing chamber. I eyed the room, looking back to him in confusion. "The hot springs? If I remember correctly, you showed me that pretty well last night."

I leaned into him, smirking as he bent down to kiss me deeply. The world around me tilted as I got lost in the taste on his lips. He pulled away far too quickly, though, laughing as I put a hand against his chest to keep from stumbling.

"No, goddess. I have something *else* to show you. Something that requires you to get ready for the day."

My face fell, the hope of sharing the hot springs with him disappearing as he let go of my hand and walked back to the door.

He threw me a wink before closing the door behind him and leaving me alone in the solitude of the bathing chamber. I waited a moment to see if he'd somehow change his mind and return. But after several moments of silence, I abandoned the idea and headed over to the hot springs. I turned the tap, watching in wonder as the water fell from the odd faucet attached to the ceiling. I let the silk dressing gown fall to the floor as I stepped into the water.

I sighed into the relief of the warmth it offered, my body more sore than I realized from the previous night's activities. I trailed my fingers over the marks Death had left on me, picturing each moment in my mind. As wonderful as the hot springs felt, I wanted nothing more than to be back in his presence, allowing him to leave new marks on my skin.

I quickly cleansed myself, letting the fragrant soap he'd left for me wash over my skin. I hesitated a moment beneath the rainfall of water before turning off the tap and stepping out of the hot springs. I dried myself with the towel he'd set out for me and ventured over to the cabinet. To my surprise, I found a fresh set of clothes hanging inside for me.

I grinned to myself as I slipped the gossamer gown on, wrapping the braided rope around my middle and securing it in place with a knot. I turned to the full-length mirror in the corner, sashaying the skirts of the gown and admiring its deep shade. It reminded me of dusk, the few moments where the light of day bled into the depth of night. Darker than twilight but not quite purple or black. Beautiful. Like Death had picked it just for me.

Letting that thought linger, I tiptoed back across the room and out into the hall. Death waited, leaning against the back of the sofa. His head turned towards me as I cleared my throat and emerged from the hallway.

"Goddess," he purred, his eyes tracing every curve of my body. He rose to meet me, hooking an arm around my back as he leaned down. "We really should be going," he whispered.

"Why?" I asked, finding it hard to focus on anything other than how close his lips were to mine in this moment.

"Because if we linger a moment longer, I'm going to drag you back to that bed and fuck you until you beg me to stop."

My heart dropped into my stomach, battling with how badly I wanted him to make good on his threat. Heat rose to my cheeks, my mind telling me I should be ashamed of how much he was turning me on right now. But something deeper in me fought back, pushing that shame out and drowning it in raw power.

Death stilled, feeling the surge of my magic, and fighting his own in response. "Not fair," he gritted out as he leaned in, taking my lower lip between his teeth. He released me, backing away suddenly.

"Let's go," he growled. He held the door open for me and I couldn't help but smirk as I walked past him, glancing down at the evident bulge straining against his pants.

Death led me out to an open-air courtyard. We stood off to the side on a stone platform, overlooking the dried, cracked earth below. Solid stone steps led up to a pitch-black throne, not unlike the obsidian stone that made up the hearth in his chambers. It looked powerful and intimidating. But as he brought me closer, I noticed the shimmering flecks and the intricate carvings—cascades of skulls, stars, moons, and suns. They were so carefully etched, bursting with delicate detailing. I reached a hand out and ran my fingers over them.

"It's beautiful," I whispered, circling the throne and finding more carvings to match on the other side. Pulling my eyes away, I looked out to the land beyond. It should have been morning, perhaps even midday at this point—but the world around us was shrouded in a deep twilight. I took a step back as my eyes adjusted to the light, seeing the buildings beyond the courtyard. Souls floated down streets and through shops, filling the air with the pleasant lull of chatter.

I eased forward, my feet stopping only when they found the top edge of a set of stairs. I couldn't believe my eyes. A whole world existed down here, a world full of content souls apparently free to wander and explore and just...exist. It wasn't all darkness and violence, as I'd always believed it to be. I watched as indistinct forms sat and ate breakfast on the patio of a nearby cafe. Another group drifted from one shop to another, quietly conversing and laughing with each other.

I looked back to Death, who was leaning against his throne with a smug look on his face. This place was brimming with *life*. I couldn't comprehend—didn't understand—how this could be. I had never ventured to the Depths. Arne had only ever reported back tales of horror— a vile, despicable place full of never-ending torment similar to what I encountered in the mortal realm. But this was peaceful, joyful even.

"A bit shocked?" Death finally mused. He came up beside me, arms clasped behind his back as he looked out over his kingdom.

"What is this?" I asked, dumbfounded.

"This, goddess, is the underworld. The afterlife." Joy radiated from him.

"I don't understand," I said, stumbling over my words as I backed away. I retreated to the cover of the stone structure, leaning on one of its pillars for support. "The Depths were supposed to be..." I trailed off. "I thought—" I shook my head in confusion.

Death followed, his demeanor annoyingly calm.

"The place we just emerged from is the Depths. It is where the damned souls are kept, where myself and the Daeomi reside.

Everything beyond…" He turned, gesturing to the world around us. "That is the underworld. Where souls deemed worthy enough get to enjoy a second chance at living."

I covered my mouth, too stunned to speak.

"I wanted to build something here, Cailli. An opportunity for an afterlife worth living. A *better* chance than many of them had in the mortal realm."

Tears sprung to my eyes. It was beautiful, wonderful. Something I should have thought of. My creation, brimming with life—just how I'd always imagined them in the mortal realm.

Death circled, coming up from behind and wrapping his arms around me. "I started building it when the mortal realm turned. When the deities retreated and the fae and mortals were left to serve themselves. There were so many souls to claim, so many that didn't deserve the harsh cruelty of the Depths." He paused. I could feel the hammering of his heart as he leaned into me. "I knew your creation deserved better. I knew it would break you to know they had nowhere else to go. So I built them something better."

He wiped away a stray tear, replacing it with a kiss to my cheek. "I built them this. For you."

He grabbed my hand, turning me towards him. His presence was overwhelming, my back bending just to look up at him. Kindness seeped into his eyes as he offered me a soft smile. He took my face in his hands, brushing away more tears with his thumbs as I lost myself to the insanity of the world around me.

"Don't cry, goddess," he whispered. "This is a good thing."

"How could I not? My entire existence I believed you to be a truly detestable being." I choked on a sob, my voice breaking. "We said such horrible things—*did* such horrible things to you, Death! And all the while, you were down here building this."

I shut my eyes, trying to gain control of the emotions coursing through me.

"Cailli, your assumptions were not misplaced. I may have spent the last several decades building this for you, but it didn't always look like this." He rested his forehead against mine. "Make no mistake, I have done horrible things. Truly vicious, vile, detestable things. I am not a good male. And those I judge unworthy are subject to an eternity of my cruelty down below."

I could feel his power writhe around us, knowing his thoughts were back in that dungeon with the fae he'd tortured until I was ready to exact my vengeance. I pressed a hand to his chest, calming the storm that was building inside him.

"I know your darkness, Death. But this? This is light. And this is something you did all on your own." I smiled up at him. "Your light, not mine."

He shook his head. "No, Divine. If it weren't for the love and light you poured into your creation, I never would have been inspired to build this."

I let him envelop me, wrapping my arms around his body and burying my face in his chest. He held me, stroking my hair as I breathed in his scent and let it calm my tears.

"Come," he whispered, finally breaking away. "Sit down." He led me away from the stairs and gestured for me to sit. My eyes went wide as I looked from him to the throne.

"No, it's yours," I argued.

"I sit there as judge and executioner. But I want you to sit there as the Divine looking over her creation. See it through my eyes, just for a moment."

I nodded hesitantly, dropping his hand and moving to the throne. I could feel his power embedded in the stone, the thrum of its strength as it vibrated through my fingers. I turned to face Death and lowered myself onto the seat. From this viewpoint, I could see the still bustling souls beyond the courtyard, full of life, even in death. But I could also see the spirits that had entered this courtyard over the centuries, that had knelt before this throne and waited to be judged. I felt the weight of the decision to allow them a second chance or to damn them to the Depths. I felt the loneliness of that duty.

I exhaled slowly, letting that weight settle over me—an eternity of impossible decisions he had to make completely on his own. It broke my heart, thinking of him upon his throne with no others to share that responsibility.

But...had my life been any different? I might have lived in the Realm of the Gods with the other deities, but my existence had been just as isolating. Just as lonely.

Death watched me as he knelt, understanding somehow where my thoughts had turned. He reached out, running his hand up my leg.

"We have both been alone for so long, goddess." He shook his head, regret shimmering in his midnight eyes. "It's not how it was meant to be. We were never meant to live separate lives, in hatred of each other."

I sat up, pulling out of his reach as I cocked my head to the side. "What do you mean?"

"Can't you feel it, Cailli?" His fingers found my leg once more, tightening their hold as an extension of his frustration. "This was not the path set out for us. We have fallen into an existence so entirely opposite of what was intended for us."

His hand slid up my leg, gripping the back of my knee and pulling me to the edge of the throne. "We may be creation and destruction. But we are also life and death, darkness and light." His other hand trailed over the hem of my dress, lifting it and draping it across my lap. "We are two sides of the same coin. Not opposites meant to live in isolation." He placed a kiss on my now exposed knee, never taking his eyes off me. "We are two cosmic forces meant to live in harmony." He kissed my other knee, centering himself between my legs. "Together."

"Death," I whispered, my voice breathy and nearly silent. "The souls, they'll see."

His eyes flicked down, a primal power raging there. Then he pulled me to his mouth. My head fell back against the throne. I could barely form the thought, barely had the ability to remember my concerns. Death feasted as if he had a hunger that had never known satisfaction. I gripped the sides of the throne, my composure impossible to maintain with the ferocity of his tongue.

Death snapped his fingers without altering his persistence against me. I forced my vision past the god on his knees before me, only to find the world beyond cloaked in shadow. We were alone in the courtyard. The realization had me crying out, finally releasing the last shred of control I was clinging to.

I was climbing, higher and higher. I couldn't focus on anything besides the feel of his punishing tongue, the waves of pleasure drowning out any lingering thought for everything he'd just shared with me. I chased those waves, splitting in two as I drove desperately over the edge of oblivion.

Just as I was sure I couldn't know a truer form of pleasure, Death retreated. Within an instant he pulled me up and bent me over his throne. Pushing the gossamer gown up, he drove his finger inside me, curving them in a wicked way that had me groaning into the stone seat. I leaned into his touch while his other hand fumbled with the fasten of his pants.

I'd barely had time to adjust to the feel of his fingers in me before he replaced them with his cock, sinking slowly in and drawing cries of pleasure from us both.

"From the first time you graced my realm, goddess, I've thought about taking you on my throne." He slammed into me with a desperate need for more.

I laughed between ragged breaths, tilting my head back to him. "And?" I asked. "Is it everything you hoped for?"

He drove himself in, grunting as he tried to control his power. "It's so much fucking better than I could have imagined."

My laugh turned into a cry as he thrust his hand into my hair, wrapping the long copper strands around his fist and pulling my head back. "There's only one thing I want to hear out of your mouth right now, goddess," he growled. "And that's my name on those pretty little lips as you come again."

I was reeling from the tremors of pleasure still rolling through my body, trying to make sense of how he expected me to come again so soon. Shadows wrapped around me in answer, one going straight to where his mouth had been moments ago, picking up that same steady rhythm. The other curled around my body, toying with my breasts and snaking over my skin in a way that had me chasing desperately after it, before it slowly retreated.

I felt its absence around me as if it were a part of me, suddenly ripped away. I opened my mouth, ready to beg for its return just as I felt its cool touch against my lower back. "Death," I whispered into the black stone surrounding me.

The shadow trailed lower, a steady pressure against me as Death guided it to where he wanted. I gasped in shock as it pressed against me, stretching that sensitive rosebud just enough to tease me. It was an entirely new sensation, the battle between fire and ice fighting to take over inside me.

"No, goddess," Death pushed back, his rhythm slowing as he leaned forward, fist still in my hair as he pulled my head back to him. "My real name."

My mind went numb, confusion taking over where desire had just been. His real name? I searched within the confines of my mind, my memories. Never in our entire existence together had I ever called him anything besides Death.

I felt his darkness penetrate my mind, his shadows slipping over my skin, a thought forming at the edge of my mind. A single word carried to me on a tendril of obsidian mist.

The name was like a key, unlocking something hidden within the deepest part of me. The fear was drowned in the rush of the memories of a life never lived, a desire never given light.

"Alistair."

I let his name radiate through me, filling every part of me until it was spilling off my lips. I cried it out as if I'd said it a million times before, as if I'd heard it every moment of my life—on the wind that passed through the sweet grass outside my window, through the rustle of the vines as I walked through the garden. It was everywhere, all around me, for every moment of my existence. I'd known it my whole life, even if I hadn't been able to remember it.

He faltered at the word that rolled off my tongue, his grip slipping in my hair as his body shuddered in answer.

"Alistair." I let the name slip through my lips again, taking advantage of his momentary lapse. I enjoyed the feel of his body's reaction against mine—the way it caused his composed rhythm to falter. He gripped my hip, one hand still firmly wrapped around my hair as he threw a newfound strength behind the shadows still working over me. I cried out, repeating his name a final time as I plummeted over the edge. My body spasmed with overwhelming waves of pleasure as he chased my release with his own, spilling into me with a roar powerful enough to shake the ground beneath our feet.

He stilled against my back, his arms falling to either side of the throne as we leaned against the black stone together. Nothing but the sound of our ragged breathing filled the air. I didn't realize his shadows were still wrapped around me until he slowly reined them back in, helping me to my feet and letting my dress fall back over my body. He fastened his own pants back into place before turning me to face him. He hooked a finger under my chin, raising my lips to his. He was gentle, soft, and torturously delicate as he kissed me.

He broke away, leaving me lightheaded and exhausted as he looked down on me. I knew he could see the hundreds of questions circling in my mind, on the tip of my tongue. He put his finger to my lips.

"There will be time to address it all, Cailli. And I vow to answer every question I can."

His finger fell from my lips, wrapping around the back of my neck as he pulled me in for one more short kiss before turning us back towards the door to the Depths.

My breath hitched as I took in the sight around us, stopping both of us in our tracks. Blossoms surrounded the courtyard, replacing the cracked and decaying earth, vining and climbing up the steps, and twining around the stone pillars. They had taken over everything in sight, aside from the throne we'd been on. My hand flew to my mouth as I turned, taking them all in. Thousands of silver orbs lit up the courtyard, the blossoms opening to reveal the special magic within. The night-blooming flowers I'd created for Death.

I looked to the sky, a sound somewhere between a laugh and a sob escaping me as I realized this had been the reason I'd made them night-blooming. Regular flowers would have never survived down here, where the sun never shone. They thrived only in darkness. "Cailli?" Death's voice was quiet, confused. "What are these?"

I spun, my eyes landing back on him. He looked just as stunned as I was. I suppressed the urge to giggle at the sight of him so caught off guard.

"I made them." I spoke softly, stopping beside the closest pillar to admire the blooms thriving there. "Before the attack with Ballam, I'd been in my garden observing my new creation. It was the night of their first bloom. My magic must have made more when we..." I trailed off as I gently ran my fingers over the petals, jostling the pollen and sending a small cloud of silver light into the air between us. Death leaned in, examining the creation in wonderment.

"Ballam loved them," I added quietly. Death's gaze met mine over the black petals, the silver orb casting a strange light over his face. A flash of grief shone in his eyes, but it was gone before I could acknowledge it.

"They are extraordinary, goddess, just like you." His concentration was focused solely on the complex blossom before him. I smiled but shook my head as I held the flower out for him to examine closer.

"No, Death, just like *you*."

His face fell, his eyes going wide as he looked from me to the flower inches from him.

"Solid, fortified exterior," I continued gently. "Soft, silky interior. Made up of all-consuming darkness, but with the purest bit of light radiating deep within."

I could see Death's throat bob in the silvery glow as he swallowed. Tears threatened to spill over his long, dark lashes.

"What do you call them?" His gaze didn't leave the flower as he spoke, his jaw tightening with the effort he was pouring into keeping his composure.

"Alistiniums," I answered without a second thought. The name had been buried within me, waiting for the perfect time to announce itself. Death's eyes shot to mine, his brow furrowed as lines of confused emotion crinkled across his face.

I leaned in, inhaling the calming scent of the flower that reminded me so much of the god standing before me—days spent beneath the cool water of a fresh spring, hints of spearmint on a cool night's breeze. I whispered the common name, letting the words carry through the space between us:

"The kiss of Death."

CHAPTER 19
Death

The low lighting of my chambers illuminated the untouched plates of steaming food. A steady fire blazed in the hearth across the room, echoed by an assortment of candles laid out on the table between us. I'd brought Cailli back here after our time together in the courtyard. My eyes drifted to the missing tome from the sisters' archives. I'd made sure to place it where she'd be able to see it, unsure how else to reveal the truth to her within the confines of the deities' magical hold. There was still so much she needed to know, so much still threatening us beyond this realm.

I bristled at the sight of it now, that tainted magic within me fighting to conceal the truth. I knew this was walking a very fine line. I may not be confessing the truth directly to her, but leaving such delicate information out openly, in hopes that she would find it... It had to be a violation of some kind. Given the pain I was feeling within me, I knew my suspicions were correct.

But tucked away in the safety of my kingdom, I couldn't find the energy to be bothered by any of it. Instead, I stared at her over the dinner one of my Daeomi had brought for us—completely entranced in her beauty.

A smile played on her soft scarlet lips. A secret battle danced behind her eyes, conflicting desires of lust and knowledge. I knew she had questions, and I wanted so badly to answer them all. But not as badly as I wanted to pin her beneath my shadows again and pour every last drop of myself into her, again and again until she begged for mercy. Judging by the way she was looking at me now though, I was almost positive she wouldn't dare beg me to stop.

"Death." Her sultry voice broke through the silence of the room, shaking me from my thoughts. I tsked, waiting for her to correct her error. She dipped her head in an attempt to hide her amusement.

"Alistair," she tried again. I leaned in, my teeth involuntarily dragging over my lower lip at the sound of my name, my true name, on her tongue.

I didn't think I'd ever get used to hearing my name on her lips. It had been centuries since it had been uttered. But her saying it now, it had to mean something—had to be a sign she was ready for the truth.

Her composure slipped, her body leaning towards mine without a second thought. Her lips parted, legs opened, a wicked kind of heat pooling in her cheeks and along her collarbone. It was only for a moment, that primal desire to be near me, with me, on me, taking over—before she shook her head, righting herself in her seat as she fixed me with a hardened stare.

"No, Death. We have too much to discuss to allow ourselves to become... distracted. Again." She turned her attention toward the plate of food in front of her, some sort of roasted meat and potatoes, using her fork to pick through the meal. "Besides, we wouldn't want all this perfectly fine food to go to waste."

I chuckled, licking my lips as I sat back in my chair and raised my glass to her. "By all means, goddess, don't let me keep you from your dinner. I'm sure you're *famished.*" Her eyes shot to mine on the last word. She held my gaze, her stubbornness threatening to take over.

"And you're not?" she challenged, gritting her teeth together.

"Oh, I'm plenty hungry." I smirked, my eyes dipping low to where the slit of her dress parted to reveal a dangerous amount of skin. Cailli dropped her fork to the table with a clatter as she let out a frustrated breath, pulling my eyes back up to hers.

My smile grew, knowing full well despite the resolve she was clinging to, there was only one thing either of us had an appetite for right now. It didn't seem to matter how much of each other we'd claimed over the last couple days. It hadn't been enough. I had a feeling it would never be. We would spend eternity chasing each other, desperate for more no matter how much the other had already given.

"Fine," she gritted out. "But we do have many things to discuss. And *that* I will not relent."

I ran my fingers absent-mindedly over the rim of my glass, appreciating the glow of her pearly skin in the firelight. I took my time, letting my eyes rake over every inch of her body before landing again on her face. "Where do you want to start, Divine?"

She closed her eyes, taking a deep breath as she tried to clear her mind. My shadows reached out, testing the boundaries I'd felt give way earlier. They slipped into her mind with frightening ease, caressing and exploring at the newfound sensation.

Her eyes snapped open. "Let's start with that."

I let my presence grow inside her, slipping through every corner of her mind.

You don't like the feel of me inside you, goddess?

My smile grew as I saw her restraint slip slightly, that other-worldly desire fighting to break through. But she caught herself, adamantly slamming down a wall and pushing me out.

"How are you doing that?" she asked, refusing to acknowledge my question.

I took a sip from my glass, cherishing the steady burn as the spirits swished through my mouth and slid down my throat. "My shadows speak to me," I finally answered. "I send them out when there's information I want and they report back to me with what they find."

She waited patiently for me to connect the dots, tapping a finger idly against her skin where her arms crossed over her chest.

"I had a theory that perhaps they'd be able to reach you within your mind, given how...*deep* our connection seems to be."

"So you didn't know you could do that?" she asked, narrowing her eyes on me.

I shook my head, taking another sip and emptying my glass. "No. But it was a delightful discovery, I will admit." I turned my attention back to her. "You didn't answer my question, though."

She cocked her head, trying to recall what I had asked. I leaned forward, letting my forearms rest against the edge of the table.

"Do you enjoy the feeling of me inside you—"

She opened her mouth to argue, but I cut her off:

"Inside your mind, I mean."

She mirrored my smirk as she watched me for a moment, considering.

"If it does not please you then I will refrain from doing it again," I added when she did not answer.

She leaned forward finally, tracing her fingers over the back of my hand. "It feels like..." She hummed as she tried to find the right wording. "The rush of water over river stones. The light of a moonbeam slipping through the darkness of night." A shadow slipped out, trailing over her bare feet beneath the table as she spoke. She didn't even flinch at the motion, but rather leaned into its touch, into my touch. Her voice lowered as she continued: "It feels as natural as breathing. Even if it may take me some time to get used to the sensation."

I stilled her fingers, taking her hand in mine and raising it to my lips. I planted a kiss there, never taking my eyes off hers. She dropped her gaze, that taunting shade of rouge returning to her cheeks. "What I don't understand..." She lightly coughed, trying to clear her throat. Her hand slipped from mine as she sat up, taking a sip of water from her glass. "...is what happened when you told me your name."

I mimicked her movement, straightening in my chair. "Elaborate, goddess."

"It was as if"—she chewed on her lower lip—"I've heard your name my whole life, Alistair. I don't know how, but it's always been there. A whisper on the wind, in the sway of the flowers in my garden. I have heard it everywhere. And yet, I couldn't remember until you spoke it. It felt like a distant dream just out of my memory's reach." Confusion clutched her mind, her eyes searching anywhere and everywhere to make sense of what she was feeling. "How is that possible?"

I let out a sigh, scrubbing a hand over my face. Things would be much less complicated if I was able to just tell her what I knew. But even after finding out the full extent of the truth, I still couldn't break that curse for her. "I will always be honest with you, Cailli. You deserve that, and so much more. But some of the questions even I can't answer." I tapped my fingers on the table, trying to figure out how to share things with her in a way that would bypass that magic.

"When I showed up in that garden, when I found Arne and Lukus attacking you and...Ballam's mutilated remains." I paused, anger writhing within me. "I whispered something to Arne. Did you hear what I told him?"

She shook her head, face drawn taut with concern.

"I told him that I finally understood the truth. And that he would never be able to claim what's mine." My eyes flicked up to hers. She watched me, patiently waiting for me to go on. But words escaped me. Seeing her here with me, in the shadows of the Depths—it was making it so painfully clear how long I'd lost her, how close I'd come to never having her... again.

I cleared my throat, suddenly overtaken by emotion. I pushed out of my chair, taking my glass. I reached out a hand for hers as well, offering to refill it. She eyed me cautiously, but didn't question the emotion so clearly rushing through me. She handed me her glass and I padded through the living space to the bar full of crystal decanters and refilled both our glasses with a healthy pour of my favorite gin.

"But what does that mean?" she called out, still sitting at the table behind me. The confession was on the tip of my tongue, an explanation for everything she ever questioned. I took a deep sip from my glass, my other hand clutching the marble countertop of the bar as I felt the deities' magic writhing inside me.

I gritted my teeth, trying desperately to fight their hold. There was nothing I wanted more than to share the truth with her, to reveal to her all that I'd discovered.

"When the realms were first made," I finally choked out. "When the cosmos bestowed power to these lands, the deities came to be. We were made for the sole purpose of creating and governing over the realms, life and death and everything in between.

"But I've been working over the last several decades to unearth… certain deceptions. I've scoured every library in every realm to decipher the truth. And what I've finally come to believe…"

I paused, the deities' magic twisting inside me like venom-laced daggers. It would break her to know the extent of the lies she'd been fed. But perhaps a breaking was necessary, in order for the light of her true strength to shine. She had proven she was ready. By punishing her own creation, by remembering my true name, by accepting me now as she believed me to be—memories or not. This time, the truth wouldn't be obscured.

"Death…" I could hear the confusion in Cailli's voice, the urgency for me to answer her fully.

"I know, I know, goddess. Just—give me a minute as I try to figure out how to say this." Even as I responded, I could feel their magic tightening its hold, forcing down my confession.

"No, Death. What is this?"

I lifted my head, turning back to the table where she sat. Relief flooded me as I saw the missing tome in her hands. Her fingers slipped over the pages, her eyes poring over its contents. I didn't respond, didn't dare interrupt for fear she'd stop reading. Cailli's eyes went wide as she took in the book's contents.

I stepped forward, slowly, tentatively. My shadows reached out to that hidden magic within both of us, a constant, suffocating presence. But for the first time in centuries, its grip had loosened.

"In the beginning, there was life and death, creation and destruction." I ventured carefully, still testing the boundaries of that magic. To my surprise, it didn't push back at my words. "You and I. Alone."

Cailli didn't speak, too stunned to comprehend what I was insinuating, so I pressed on as I made my way back to the table.

"The others were not deities. At least, not at first. They were high-reigning fae who got too power-hungry and too ambitious. They did not hold positions of power over the realms as we did."

Cailli shook her head, trying to make sense of my words. "No, that can't be. I would remember if it were so."

"You wouldn't," I argued, lowering my voice in an effort to make it less disarming as I took my seat. Even now I could feel the anger at what they'd done rushing through my veins, making my shadows grow. "I haven't been able to find any mention of their existence in the early archives. The deities, yes, but no mention of them by name or position. It's like, one day they just showed up. No explanation from whence they came or who they are. And until now, our origin records were missing too many details to make sense. Like maybe something all along had been missing, hidden away or overwritten."

"Until now?" she asked, glancing down at the book between us.

I took a deep breath, incapable of focusing on anything besides the disbelief and horror in her golden eyes.

"I caught one of the sisters trying to hide something within the mortal realm just after your first visit to the Depths. Karmi. When I confronted her about it, she offered this to me. The sisters have begun to piece together the same thing I have. Theora discovered it, hidden away among Lukus' chambers and wanted it taken to a safer place, in case the other deities realized it was missing."

"What is it?" She ran her hand over the solid, ancient cover.

"The first account of fated mates."

Her eyes flicked up to meet mine, her fingers stalling against the spine.

"Our love story."

Cailli gasped, pulling her hand back from the tome. Her eyes searched mine for a moment before hastily grabbing the book and tearing into its pages once more. "I don't understand," she muttered as she flipped through each page, skimming the records within.

"The records have been tampered with to conceal our origins. Its contents may have been altered, but this story...it's ours, goddess. The true history of our love, our existence."

I leaned in towards her, grasping her hand firmly now as I tried to keep her here in this moment with me and out of her own mind. She pulled her eyes from the text to find mine. The golden glow of her eyes burned brighter against the tears threatening to spill over her lashes.

"Our story has persisted through time, Cailli. It has unfolded over and over again amongst the realms."

Distorted, corrupted memories ran wild in her mind despite my words. My presence in her mind could feel their lies writhing—the stronghold of their magic still lingering within her, trying to beat the rising truth into submission and cloak it under the mask of their power.

"There's a reason my name feels so familiar to you. Why, despite everything that's been pitted against us, you were still incapable of denying these feelings for me."

I dropped her hand, opening the tome on the table between us once more.

"Let me show you," I pleaded.

Her eyes shone with fear and unshed tears. But she nodded anyway, desperate to make sense of the chaos raging in her mind. Shadows unfurled from the tome, surrounding us in darkness and transporting us through time.

"Every set of fated mates that have ever existed in the mortal realms is a mirror of what we once were, what we are still meant to be." The shadows shifted and morphed from one scene to another. Nature and beauty and love collided to reveal their truth to her.

"Every piece of your creation was made out of our love. Every grand mountain, every starry sky. They were your love letters to me. You said you'd heard my name whispered on the wind throughout your whole life? It's because you poured your love into each and every part of your creation. Love is what inspired you to create in the first place."

Magical mountains surrounded us, filling the room until it was impossible to feel like we were anywhere but in their midst. Then the shadows shifted again, changing to a peaceful, expansive meadow. We stood amongst the tall grass, looking up at endless constellations written throughout the cosmos. The shadows shifted once more, revealing the fae kingdoms, far before their downfall. When they were thriving and full of life.

"Those love stories filling my library? They all point back to one thing. To us. You created an entire existence of creatures to experience what we had. Because you believed all should feel that kind of love."

I reached out, brushing a stray tear from her cheek.

"You asked me why I collect those books? It's because I knew there was something about them, a deeper meaning I was meant to unearth. They are our story. They are *all* our story. Time after time, again and again. The cosmos have set in motion a ripple effect of our love to help bring us back to this moment, to help us find each other again and again. Because our love is something special, our power unmatched when we are one. As it should be."

I breathed a sigh of relief, a weight lifted from my chest as I was able to finally reveal the truth to her. This had existed in my mind for far too long, but hearing my own words now, seeing her take in the full extent of the truth I was sharing...I had waited a lifetime for this moment.

She was frantic, panicked, as she tried to process all that I was sharing. My heart hurt for her; my spirit *ached* as I watched her entire world come crashing down. She knew—deep down, somewhere and somehow—she knew I was right. She'd known it from the second I'd uttered my name into her mind. It had been a key, unlocking a flood of long-lost answers to questions she hadn't even begun to ask. But knowing it and accepting it were two different things.

"They have done so much to keep us apart, used magic and deception and any means necessary to ensure we kept our distance. I don't know how they did it. I don't know how they've blocked our memories for so long. I'm still searching for answers. But they are *evil*, Cailli, and they've convinced you that you are powerless, defenseless—less than. If you could only see what I see, goddess. You are so much *more*."

I closed my eyes, willing peace within her mind, a calm rolling across a stormy sea. I felt the sigh of relief from her body as she gave way to my presence within her. I let that relief radiate, build, and settle into the dark recesses of her mind.

Spurred on by my newfound freedom, I told her of the sheer volume of the ancient texts and tomes I'd scoured over my lifetime. I told her about the archives Ballam and I had searched in our short time amidst their realm, how there was such a blatant lack of history for the others. I told her of the deception I'd observed from them, the odd behaviors and questionable conduct that led me to believe in their guilt.

Scene after scene, vision after vision played out amidst the shadows surrounding us. It was a lifetime of lies and dirty magic used against us. A lifetime of insecurities and isolation at their hand. I felt her spirit break, felt the hot, angry tears free falling down her face as she took it all in, never once asking me to stop.

When I'd shown her everything, the shadows dispersed. A heavy silence fell over the room as she sat with the truth that had finally been revealed.

"I am so sorry, goddess." My voice shook, a mixture of pain and rage. "If I had known sooner, if I had been able to get through to you before now, I would have." I ran my thumb over her soft cheek, now wet with tears. "Please believe me when I say that I have spent a lifetime trying to make my way back to you."

She sobbed, falling out of her chair and into my arms. I could feel her pain, not just see it or sense it, but actually *feel* it in my chest, my bones. My shadows danced around the room in response, antsy for an escape, for somewhere to land. I held her as she cried, stroking the silken copper strands of her hair.

"How could I have been so blind?" Her words were muffled as she spoke into the fabric on my chest. My hand stilled, straining to tamp down on the power building beneath my skin. I loosed a deep breath, grabbing her by the shoulders and raising her so that our eyes met.

"No, goddess. Do not blame yourself. They did this, not you."

She shook her head, refusing to meet my gaze. "If I had been stronger, if I had paid more attention. Death, we should have lived an eternity together." Her voice broke, hands shaking as she steadied herself against my chest. "My entire creation is suffering because they locked me away in that damned realm. All because they couldn't stand the thought of having less power than us, because they wanted what we had."

I ran my hands up her arms, trying desperately to absorb the power I could feel radiating within her, if only to help calm her.

"I know, Cailli—"

"We have to do something." Her body stilled. Her fidgeting stopped as her eyes focused finally on mine. A wild determination set across her face. "We have to take care of this, Death. They cannot get away with this. They cannot continue to rule."

"Trust me, goddess," I soothed. "They won't get away with this. But we cannot react yet, we need to be smarter than them. And rushing back to their doorstep on a wave of anger will only give them the upper hand."

She deflated against me, sinking against my chest as she pulled herself fully into my lap.

"So what, we just stay here then? Let them continue with whatever it is they're doing, plotting and planning against us?"

Even as she said it, my skin heated. My power cried out for vengeance, seeing how deeply they'd hurt her. I knew it would not be easy restraining myself. If it were only myself to worry about, I'd be hurling myself through realms and burning down their palace without a second thought. But I had to be stronger, smarter. For her. I would not allow them to harm her any more than they already had. And that would require meticulous planning.

I wrapped my arms around her, noting the way her head tucked against my shoulder and chin as if she was made to fill that space. Everything about her fit so perfectly against me. For what felt like the millionth time in my life, I scolded myself for not realizing our purpose sooner.

"My Daeomi are scattered amongst the mortal realm. They will report back if the other deities make any moves that we need to be aware of. And in the meantime, we'll form a plan of action. Think things through before we make our next move."

She didn't answer for a long time, silence filling the room around us. Her breaths calmed, her body relaxing against me. Her tears had stopped falling—but it didn't stop my anger from growing, my chest still wet with their sorrow. Before I took their lives, I would give them a lash for every tear they'd ever made her shed.

"Okay," she finally relented. She laced her arms behind my back, burrowing deeper against me. "Take me to bed, Death. I don't think I can spend another moment thinking on this tonight."

I wrapped my arms around her, standing as I pulled her close against my chest. She weighed nothing in my arms, her presence only lifting the burdens I typically carried. Her breath hitched at the motion, surprise swirling in those beautiful golden eyes.

"It would be my pleasure, goddess."

CHAPTER 20
The Divine

I pored over the text before me, frantically reading as fast as I could. I had already read it from cover to cover last night. Twice more this morning. And still, I couldn't get enough of its contents. Death's footfall pulled my attention away from the book in my hands. He made his way back towards me from his library, a fresh stack of texts and tomes in his arms. Books already covered every available surface before us. I'd insisted on going over every piece of information he'd collected since he started hunting for answers.

"This should be the last of them," he said as he dropped the new stack on the floor beside the low table in the sitting room. I stretched my back, rolling my shoulders as I prepared to dive back into the book in my lap. I'd chosen to start with the book Karmi had given Death. It seemed to be the most impactful, directly relating to both me and Death.

The more I read, the more my mind reeled. Wave after wave of emotion crashed over me. Grief, excitement, hatred; pure, agonizing sadness. But more than any of them, the one that shone through the brightest was love. Reading about a life I still couldn't quite remember was jarring, but I found the same light and tenderness I had discovered within Death himself these past few weeks within the book's pages.

I was grateful to Karmi for sharing the tome with us, even if I was aggravated that neither Death nor the sisters had chosen to share these suspicions with me earlier. I reached over to the low-rise table, picking up a still steaming cup of coffee and taking a sip.

"Take a break, Cailli. Eat some breakfast, stretch your legs."

I glared up at him, not missing the way he winked at me while making his last suggestion. I knew exactly what kind of *stretching* he had in mind. But I wasn't ready to forgive him yet. Not until I fully understood everything he knew.

"Alright, well, if you won't take a break, will you at least let me help you? You've barely said two words to me since you started digging into all of this." He made his way over to where I sat, moving an assortment of handwritten notes and reference tomes I'd laid out across the velvet sofa.

"It's not my fault I have so much catching up to do," I shot back, flipping to the next page of the book in my hands.

Death paused mid-sip of his own coffee. "Careful how you speak to me, goddess, before I have to teach that mouth a lesson."

"Unlikely," I mumbled as I tossed my hair over my shoulder, returning my gaze to the book in my lap. A shadow shot out, pulling the text from my hands before I could grab hold of it. My eyes narrowed on Death, anger seething in my veins as my power grew within me.

"I'm not in the mood for your games, Alistair." I threw my power behind his name, knowing it would drive him crazy. My lips twitched with amusement as I noticed the way he shifted in his seat.

"I promise you, Cailli, this isn't a game to me."

He went back to sipping on his coffee but left a shadow outstretched, wrapping around my ankles and tracing patterns up my legs. I folded my arms across my chest, tapping my fingers impatiently against my arm as I waited for him to return my book. When he didn't, I let out a frustrated grunt and picked up another tome close by.

The room exploded in shadow, the dark mist cloaking everything in sight. All sources of light were snuffed out, plunging me into the deep black and disorienting me completely. I grabbed onto the sofa, trying to ground myself.

Death's voice carried through the shadows. It was everywhere, surrounding me.

"Don't test me. There is nothing that I'd like to do more than drag you back to my bed and show you exactly how I expect to be revered."

I scoffed, peering through the darkness to try and find his physical form. "Does reverence not go both ways? I'm not feeling very revered right now. Why should I show you that respect when I haven't experienced it myself?"

I was only met with silence. I turned my head slowly, trying to get my bearings in the sudden pitch-black of the room. The shadows undulated around me. I couldn't see their motion, couldn't see anything at all, but I could feel the way they moved around me. It stretched to fill the space, teasing me as it skittered along my skin.

It was as if the air itself were alive, possessed by shadows I could not only feel touching every inch of my body, but could breathe in with each rise and fall of my chest.

"Forgive me, goddess." Death's words made me jump, the feel of his breath on my neck startling me as he leaned over me from behind. He'd moved so effortlessly, disrupting none of the books and parchment surrounding us.

"I never meant to hurt you." His fingers trailed slowly up my arm, causing me to break out in gooseflesh. His touch was so soft, so delicate. "You mean more to me than any other thing in this world, Cailli. In all the worlds. And I spent centuries trying to find my way back to you. Can you understand how I needed to be careful not to ruin that? How scared I was that revealing myself in the wrong time would set me back a lifetime?"

My mind drifted back to the not-so-distant past when I'd thought Death was vile. I'd held so much disdain for him. Even being in his presence had been nearly impossible to take. I understood now why that was. It wasn't hate I'd sensed but passion, lust—a carnal call to be with one another disguised within the corrupting magic of the other deities.

His fingers made their way up my body, landing at the nape of my neck and wrapping around my hair as he angled my head back. If I could see, I knew I'd be looking up into his eyes. But only thick mist filled my vision.

"But even when I wanted to, I couldn't speak the truth until you opened that gate. Until you remembered it for yourself—breaking their hold on you. You let me in, Cailli. You remembered. And that made the way for me to reveal the truth to you fully."

The more he spoke, the more my body melted against his. He'd had no other option but to wait for me to remember, to break that hold within my own mind. But I had so much anger in my heart for the time we lost together. And I didn't know how to handle that kind of rage. I had never experienced something like that before.

I reached up, finding his face in the darkness and pulling him to my lips. He kissed me deeply, the darkness of the room slowly residing as he did. When I pulled away, the room was back to normal.

"Alright," I relented. "Walk me through it." I held his face to mine as I spoke, his powerful form bending over mine as he wrapped his arms around me. We locked eyes for a moment longer before he broke away and started sifting through the stacks of books.

"You understand now that the other deities are nothing more than false gods, yes?" he asked as he searched, then handed me a particularly thick tome. I nodded, even though his eyes were not on me.

"Now, as I said, I do not have all the answers. The only explanation I have come to is that they snaked their way into the Realm of the Gods long ago. They got brave, found ways to harness more power, and eventually became what they are now."

He added a couple more tomes to my lap before grabbing a stack of his journals and settling back on the sofa beside me.

"From what I can tell based on the tomes I've laid out for you—what you can see I've theorized in my notes—their deceit was dependent upon keeping us separated, at odds."

I skimmed over his journals, noting the frantic markings on each page. I couldn't help but imagine Death holed up in his library for years by himself, trying to work out the truth he was sharing with me now.

"Goddess, they have tricked us. They have kept us separated, feeding us lies for *centuries*. Because they knew if we were together, there'd be no stopping what our power could do. There'd be no stopping us from shutting them out and exposing their deceit."

My heart broke, thinking of how long he'd been forced to live with this truth alone—all the while he was trying to find a way to get through to me. I might have been hurting now, but he'd been living with this, alone and isolated, for so long.

"How could they even accomplish that?" I asked, unable to look him in the eye from the guilt I felt.

Death didn't answer for a long while, his mind deep in thought as he rubbed his chin.

"I haven't been able to work that out yet," he finally answered, sitting back and dropping some loose parchment on the sofa between us. "Their magic has kept a hold on our memories, controlling what we could remember and when. And obviously keeping us from speaking to each other about this. All I know is over the years I recall having moments of deep clarity and moments of utter confusion."

He stared a few more moments at the papers between us, picking up one and reading over it before huffing out a laugh. "There were some days when I'd come home from a council meeting to my scribblings and research spread throughout the library, honestly wondering if I'd gone mad. I can't even remember writing some of these notes."

He peeked up at me over the parchment in his hands, a devious smile growing across his face.

"Nor could I believe in a life with you."

"What?" I scoffed. "Were our council meetings *that* unbearable that you couldn't stand the thought of being in love with me?"

His chuckle was low, dark as he bit down on his lower lip. "On the contrary, goddess. I couldn't fathom a world where you'd entertain a life with me. Especially not after how you treated me with such disdain."

Heat rose to my cheeks. My body clenched, the cold of his shadows now dancing around me. Embarrassment and guilt fought to win within my mind. I couldn't even argue back, because he was right. It had taken him whisking me away to the Depths to get me to realize I'd been wrong about him.

A shadow reached out, lifting my chin to meet his gaze.

"Do not blame yourself, Cailli. None of this was your fault."

A tear escaped my lashes, rolling slowly down my cheek before his shadow slipped up and brushed it away. I leaned into its touch, cherishing the cool feeling along my heated cheeks.

"Besides," Death added, throwing me a wink. "I rather enjoyed the game. Seeing how riled up you became just by my mere presence was more than enough inspiration to keep me going. And imagining how fun that fiery spirit would be bound in my shadows was enough to get me through another century if need be."

I clutched the cushion I'd been leaning on, tossing it at a very smug-looking Death. We both broke out in laughter, as he wrapped his shadows around me and tugged me into his embrace. We settled back against the sofa, silence falling over us as we looked out over the wide array of records and tomes.

"So what now?" I asked, the weight of all this knowledge finally starting to settle in.

"Now? We plan. We prepare for a fight." He wrapped a finger around my chin and brought my gaze up to meet his. "And we don't allow them to steal a single moment more of our time together."

I offered him a small smile, letting my hand traces circles against his chest. "Do you have one? A plan?"

His own smile fell slightly, taking his eyes off me to look out the far window across his chambers. "Nothing for certain. But I think we start by continuing your training. Learn how to grow your power and really test its limits."

I suppressed the urge to shudder, the memory of that awful fae guard shooting through my mind. My power surged in response, the room around us suddenly illuminated in a golden glow. Death's darkness grew in answer, reaching out and swirling with the rays of light.

"Besides..." Death whispered softly into my hair as we watched our power dance through the air.

To my surprise, two small tendrils of shadow wrapped around my palms. I closed my eyes, relishing in the cool, icy feel of them on my skin. I looked down to my palms when they cleared, stunned to find the marks they left behind: an inky black, blazing sun on one palm and a delicate star-dusted moon on the other.

I raised my palms in pure astonishment. He'd told me at one time that I'd know it if he were claiming me. And now he had. After everything we'd discussed, after everything he'd shown me, it was time for him to claim what was his, as I claimed what was mine. I was the light to his darkness, and he was the destruction to my creation. We could not have one without the other. And he'd mark me till the end of time, just so that we'd never lose sight of each other again.

"I'm not quite ready to share you with the world again."

My shock turned to amusement as my huffed laugh broke through the quiet of the sitting room. "Is that so, Alistair?"

"Oh, goddess," he whispered, breathing me in as he buried his face in my hair and whispered into my ear. "I'm just getting started."

CHAPTER 21
The Divine

I knelt on the floor of Death's library, hands fastened behind my back by one of his shadows. More trailed over me, forming a makeshift harness around my chest, my breasts. It had been two days since we spoke about the deities. Everything Death had shown me still circled in my mind. A life I never got to live, a purpose I still hadn't been able to fulfill. This place, these worlds...they were meant to be so much more. Perhaps it was not my fault that the deities had deceived me, trapping me with their magic and lies. But I couldn't shake the feeling that some of the blame still fell on me.

Death had been as much of a victim as I had, yet he'd been able to see past it. Fight his way out of their deception. He'd spent decades trying to uncover their secrets. And when he finally had, he made his way back to me. That was so much more than I could say for myself.

"You're retreating again, Cailli," Death scolded as he circled the library, making his way around me so he could see his binding skills from every angle. I bowed my head, trying to let my troubled thoughts slip away. I focused on this moment, and the moments we'd shared just before when Death had made me come—first with his fingers, then with his tongue. My lips tipped up at the corner as desire pooled in my core. I wanted to feel him again. I wanted to make up for centuries of wasted time, for the passion and perfection we should have been living in.

"My apologies, Alistair," I answered, my head still bowed to hide the smile that now ravaged my features. I couldn't help but notice what using that word did to him, his body's automatic arousal at hearing his name that hadn't been uttered for centuries. The shadows binding me constricted in response.

"You're mocking me, goddess." He bent behind me so that his lips brushed over my ear. "And I will not hesitate to show you how much I do not tolerate being teased."

I leaned back, needy for more of his body on mine. "Is that a threat?" I breathed out, letting my head fall against his chest behind me. "Or a promise?"

He righted himself, throwing off my balance and almost sending me careening backwards. A shadow caught me, returning me to my position on my knees.

I craved the pressure, the way the bindings tightened against my skin. I would take any punishment he served me and would beg for more. I flexed against the shadows at my wrists, relishing in the feel of their hold on my skin. So much had happened in the last few days. Power I didn't even know I was capable of was coming forth, revealing another side to me. The more darkness Death revealed to me, the freer I felt my light become. I let that light forth, my skin glowing with a golden hue and stopping Death in his tracks.

I smiled as I was rewarded with more shadows lacing around my calves, my thighs, knotting together to hold me in place.

"See how much your power affects me, goddess? See how strong a grasp you have on me? Your power...your being has me in a chokehold." He spoke through gritted teeth as squatted down just in front of me. He ran his cool fingers over my heated skin, letting them dip low. I moaned against the feel of his hand, demanding more as I rode his fingers. He chuckled darkly, his eyes heavy with lust as he watched me grinding against him.

"You may be beneath my bindings, Cailli. But you hold all the power here."

"So give me more," I panted.

His eyes darkened as he withdrew his fingers, holding them up to glisten in the firelight from the hearth. "In due time, goddess." He brought his fingers to his lips, licking the length clean before bringing his lips to mine. His tongue darted into my mouth, filling me with my own taste. The action should have repulsed me, vile and dirty. But it only deepened the need between my legs, my back arching to reach up to where he bent over me.

He broke away, leaving me panting and desperate.

"You're being cruel," I called out, groaning in frustration.

"I am teaching you patience," he replied, circling me again. As he made his way around me, I heard the rustle of his pants dropping to the floor. When he was within my view once more, he was fully bare and ready to take me.

"Now, Divine, I think it's time for you to show me some reverence." He stepped up to me as his words washed over me, wrapping around me just as his shadows had. "It seems I've been the only one to kneel at your altar. It only seems fair you return the gesture."

"Is that so?" I quipped, amusement seeping into my smile.

"I am a god, afterall," he mused. "Don't I deserve to be worshiped, too?"

I bowed my head in a mocking gesture, making the motion as dramatic as I could—given the restraints still digging into me. His growl vibrated through the small library, his tone drifting from amusement to something darker.

"What did I say about mocking me, goddess?"

He didn't wait for me to respond as he grabbed my hair and forced my head up, his cock mere breaths away from my face. My lips parted, my mouth watering at the sight of him so close to me. I thought of all the ways I wanted to worship him, all the places I wanted to let my lips and tongue wander to show him just how much I needed him. His jaw relaxed, his lips hinting at a smile as he looked down on me.

That's much better. I was suddenly aware of his presence in my mind, somehow not having noticed when he'd entered.

"Not fair." I pursed my lips, pouting.

His fingers brushed over my hair, lacing into the strands at the nape of my neck and holding me in place. I was rendered utterly helpless. My hands, my legs, my head pinned beneath the mercy of his control. And it didn't frighten me in the least. Staring up at the face of Death, I was suddenly struck by how little fear radiated through me. A rush of excitement and thrill, yes. But any fear I had once held for the god had long since melted to give way to something else, something more powerful, more consuming.

I closed my eyes, concentrating my power through the room as tendrils of my golden light reached out. They crept up his legs, washing over his body in a wave of love and joy. They flooded his body, his mind with the warmth of midsummer's sunlight. He closed his eyes, letting the magic take over him. It was a sight to behold: the face of Death, Ruler of the Underworld, basking in sunshine, a smile creeping over his face.

"I will worship you every day, Alistair." I whispered into the space between us. "I want nothing else but this. Always and forever this." I bowed my head again, his grasp having gone loose in my hair. This time, there was no mockery in my movements, my tone. Now that I had him, I couldn't imagine spending a single day without him by my side. And I would spend as much time as it took to help him see that he was a god deserving of worship and reverence. His darkness was ever present, but I would show him that I could see his light too, that I believed in his ability to be good and just. Even if he didn't believe it for himself.

That was why we worked so well together. We were balance. We offered each other what the other needed. He was my mirror, to show me the strength he could see in me. To help me remember my purpose and my power and to remind me that I was never alone. And I was his safe space, where he could let his mask slip and allow himself to be vulnerable. To understand that not all days had to be full of darkness—and even when they were, I could help bear that burden with him.

I knew by the way he dropped to his knees before me that he'd heard my thoughts, felt their meaning as his presence was still in my mind. He hooked a finger under my chin, slowly raising my gaze to his.

"Cailli." His breath was warm and inviting as it brushed over my skin. "You are—quite simply—my everything. I will never understand why we were made for each other, because I do not deserve you."

I nuzzled my head against his cheek, hating that he could ever think he didn't deserve me. "No, Death, it is I who does not deserve you. You have spent a lifetime trying to right my wrongs, to be what I could not be for my creation. And even now you have helped me discover who I truly am, shown me the extent of my power. I have done nothing to deserve you."

His hands cupped my face, moving me so that our noses were practically touching. "Divine, you *never* have to do anything to deserve my love. It flows freely for you. No matter what you have done or may still do. My love will always be there for you whenever you want to accept it." His lips brushed my forehead, my nose, exploring the dips and curves of my face. "You have endured so much, Cailli. It is time for you to rest now. Let me be your rest, goddess."

I pinched my eyes shut, trying to keep the tears pricking to life contained. I tried to bury my head against his chest, but he held me firm, his lips finding mine.

"Don't retreat. Don't hide. Let those emotions flow," he whispered between kisses. Tears ran hot down my cheeks as I parted my lips for him. Anger and grief and lust and desire mixed together within me, spurring me forward. He deepened our kiss, brushing tears from my cheeks as his tongue chased mine. It was the oddest sensation, letting myself feel that pain even as we pursued each other.

His shadows tightened against my skin as if to remind me that I was still bound beneath his restraints. His hand found purchase in my hair once more, balling into a fist and pulling at the delicate strands. With each new action, I could feel the grief and pain slipping away—not getting buried or pushed aside but rising to the surface and flowing out. Whatever he was doing to me, it was allowing me to let go.

A foreign feeling overcame me, pulling me from this moment with Death. My mind body went cold as I tried to fight through the sea of distance that was suddenly growing between us.

"Death," I choked out. "Wait."

His head rose, his binding dissipating without a second thought, surrounding us in a chilly obsidian mist. Gone was any hint of desire in his dark eyes. Only concern shone from them as his gaze pored over me.

"What is it?"

I was here in this room with him, but in my mind it felt as if I was forever away, calling out to him and fighting desperately to find my way back.

"Something's happened." I could barely recognize my own voice. "The Realm of the Gods, something's changed." I rose to my feet. I couldn't see what I was doing, my vision blurred and concentrated somewhere else.

"What can you sense?" He followed in my wake, no more than a heartbeat behind me.

"I—I can't tell but—" I keeled over, doubling at the hips in pain. He caught me before I hit the ground. I fought through the haze in my mind, finding his eyes. "We must go back."

"Cailli." Death's voice was low, his tone a warning. "We need to think about this."

"No!" I shouted, finding the strength to stand again. "No, Death. I can't wait. The pull is too strong. And if they are making moves against my creation, against you? I cannot hide here any longer. Something has changed, I can feel it through every part of me. I need to know what they are doing, what they might—" My words cut off, choked out by the sound of a sob as I crashed against his chest again. I wrapped my arms around him, my mind reeling from whatever it was sensing in the other realm. "I have to go," I whispered into his bare chest. "I don't have a choice."

"I know, goddess," he whispered back, leaning his head against mine and planting a kiss on the crown of my head. "But we go together, okay? We do this together."

I nodded quickly. I couldn't imagine it any other way. He held me for a moment longer before turning to the bundle of clothing he'd dropped on the floor. He handed me my dress, helping me slip it over my head before pulling his pants on and fastening them. He slipped a tunic over his head as he walked to the doorway. His hand paused on the doorknob, reaching back to take mine.

"I don't know what we will find on the other side, Cailli. But stay with me. No matter what, stay with me."

"Of course," I answered, coming up beside him and lacing my arms around his torso. "I am yours, Death, always and forever yours."

His eyes searched mine for a long moment, finally giving me a tight nod as he looked back to the doorway.

"Always and forever yours," he echoed. He turned the knob, the thick black of his shadows spreading across the doorway and obscuring our view. My body pulled me forward, urging me to step through worlds and back into the Realm of the Gods, but I held fast as I waited for him to make the first move. He let loose a deep breath as he looked back to me.

"Together," he said. And that is exactly how we stepped through the cloud of darkness.

Together.

CHAPTER 22
The Divine

My vision clouded as we walked between worlds, my stomach turning with the effort it took to get back to the Realm of the Gods. Something didn't feel right. I lost my direction, my head spinning as I tried to determine backward from forward, up from down. I coughed through the black mist, my feet finally landing on the soft grass of the place I once called home. I fell to my knees, breathing heavily as I tried to still my spinning head.

My vision cleared slowly, the world around me finally coming into focus. The palace was up ahead, my garden just to the right. It looked the same as the day I'd left it. I couldn't help but wonder if Ballam's body was still within the garden walls. I sucked in deep breaths through my nose, trying to find the strength to stand again.

"Death," I called out, reaching back for him. He had spent his entire existence doing this, but I was still trying to get used to walking between realms.

"Cailli," he responded. But something wasn't right. His voice was weakened, distant. Fear sparked in my chest as I spun around and clambered to my feet.

"Alistair," I whispered, rushing to the portal. There he was—exactly where I'd expected him to be. But he was still shrouded in shadows, still standing in the doorway between realms. "What are you doing?" Fear seeped into my voice, panic setting in.

"I can't," he said, his voice straining as he tried to move forward. I raised my hand to the doorway, feeling the barrier between our worlds. It was solid, impenetrable. I gasped, my hands going to my mouth in horror. Death was fighting, banging, trying with everything he had to get through. To get to me. But the barrier wouldn't give.

"Divine."

The icy voice sent a chill down my spine as I spun around to see Arne slink out of the nearby trees.

"So nice of you to join us again. In your rightful place."

I bit down, anger seething into every part of me.

"Arne, what is this?" I asked, gesturing to the warding—even though I already knew. "What have you done?"

Arne clasped his hands behind his back as he paced around me. Sheathed at his belt was the same blade he'd shown me in the garden. The one that killed Ballam. I kept my eyes on it as he moved.

"You didn't give us the opportunity to speak with you after that unfortunate occurrence in the gardens." His hand waved absent-mindedly towards the palace. My vision went red at his nonchalant tone, acting as if the loss of Ballam's life was no more than a small disagreement between friends. "So I summoned you—after using the depthhound's blood to alter the wardings for our realm, of course. Did Death tell you his own blood runs through the veins of those despicable creatures? Well, like father, like son, I suppose."

He chuckled, as if he didn't notice the anger pouring out of me. "We had to get you back here somehow, so we could discuss these matters and put this situation to bed." He leveled his gaze over my shoulder, past me to the deity on the other side of the portal. "Alone."

"Arne, enough!" I shouted, my temper rushing out of me like a fanned flame. I stomped towards him, Death's protests ringing out behind me. "I know what you did. I know what you've been hiding from me, that you've been keeping us apart because it was me and Death who were meant to rule over these realms. Not all of us together, not *you*." I planted my feet before him, breath ragged. I leveled my gaze, holding my ground.

He raised an eyebrow, looking between me and where Death stood still hovering between worlds. He sighed, rubbing his fingers over his brow. "I don't know what this parasite has been telling you..." He stepped forward, reaching a hand out for my arm, but I jerked backwards, avoiding his touch. He put his hands up at my motion, still stepping towards me as he spoke: "But he's been deceiving you. You are one of us, Divine, just as we are one with you. If there is anyone who has inserted themselves where they don't belong, it is *him.*" He sneered at Death over my shoulder.

"Liar!" I screamed, my rage reaching new heights. It hadn't just been Death's word. His name, his *being*, had unlocked something within me. Bringing to life some old prophecy of what we were always meant to become. I'd confirmed it for myself, reading through the scribes' record over and over again the past few days. It was our story, through and through. There was no going back, no redoing whatever had been undone within me. My eyes were open now and I would not spend another moment pretending to be blind to their deception.

"Liar?" Arne echoed. "My dear Divine, it was with great effort that we found a way to break you from Death's shadows and deceit. Now you've gone and gotten all confused listening to his trickery."

Our argument had pulled the others from the palace—Lukus and Estrid taking their places beside Arne. My mind barely registered the sisters lingering in the distance. I found myself hoping, praying that they were finally ready to reveal what they knew and put an end to this as well.

"Come home with us, let us help you understand the truth."

I looked into the eyes of each deity, finding nothing but callousness there. Whatever facade they were trying to put forth, it was failing. I could see right through them.

"No." I shook my head, taking a step back. "No, I'm not going anywhere with you. Let the wardings drop, let me back to him."

"He belongs down there," said Arne. "Alone. We've let him wander the realms for far too long. It is time we restore order, Divine."

"Let. Him. Go," I warned, lowering my voice.

"We are doing this *for you*," Arne insisted. He took a step forward, causing me to retreat. Death's voice called out behind me, a string of warnings and curses to keep my distance, to return to him. But I'd felt that barrier as much as he had. There was no going back to the Depths. Not while they had it warded.

"Undo it," I said, raising a hand to keep Arne back. "Now."

Estrid barked out a laugh, slinging her curved form against Lukus. "Or what, Divine? You'll bury us in flowers?"

Lukus sniggered, but Arne didn't take his eyes off me.

"Divine," the God of Power chided. "*Cailli.*"

I narrowed my gaze at him for using the nickname I detested hearing on his lips. It did nothing to deter him as he closed the distance between us. Death's yells picked up behind me, joined only by the sound of his fists and shadows banging against the wards. Arne's eyes flicked to him for only a moment.

"He doesn't belong here," he continued. "It's our job to keep you safe, keep you pure. And he"—he pointed a finger at Death—"He is corruption."

"He is balance!" My voice rang out around us, power expanding into the words. The trees shook, birds took flight, and the insects stilled. Even Death fell silent at the strength I'd let slip out. "You..." I argued, hate spurring me forward, "*You* are corruption." A twisted smile slithered across my lips as I raised my hands out around me. "And luckily for me, you've trapped my balance in another realm, leaving me entirely free to right this wrong myself."

Arne's face fell, confusion and something akin to fear washing over him as he saw me—finally saw me—for all I was worth. The sky darkened, the wind swirling around us as the ground rumbled with my power. Behind him, Lukus and Estrid froze, fear-stricken and completely useless. They stumbled, trying to keep their footing on the shifting grass. Arne took a step back—one singular step. That was all he had time for as my roots burst forth, splitting earth and rock, wrapping around muscle and bone, finding purchase around the three deities before me.

They fell to their knees, tangled in the roots wrapping around their wrists, their legs— holding them in place. I let one last root slip over their chests, wrapping around their throats and tightening just enough to pull from them a chorus of strangled gasps.

"Tell me the truth. Now." I curled my fingers into my palms, giving a tug on the roots around their throats to deepen my demand. Terror filled their eyes, but none of them spoke. I waited, tightening my hold on them with every passing moment.

"You don't want to share? That's fine." My bare feet padded on upturned earth as I brought myself before Estrid. If any of them had ever been my friend, it was her. But looking into her eyes now, I understood that there was never an ounce of friendship between us.

She squirmed beneath my roots, the rough wood cutting into that flawless skin of hers. "Cailleach, please," she begged, tears filling her dark brown eyes. "We are friends, are we not? I don't know what he's told you, but it's not the truth. We are your family, not—" Her words cut short, the air between us filling with a fine red mist. My roots went lax, her body falling at my feet, tongue clutched firmly in the root that had been wrapped around her throat. I wouldn't allow another lie to slip from it, even if I had to rip it out myself to do so.

I turned away from her writhing body, leaving her to choke on her own blood as I stepped up to Lukus next. Gurgled cries surrounded us as I knelt over Lukus's face. He didn't take his eyes off me, that same crooked grin he always wore still plastered to his face. But God of War and Mischief or not, even he couldn't maintain that unbothered facade. Not with the sickening cries for help coming from his lover bleeding out on the grass beside him.

"Stop this," he finally growled. "This isn't you, Cailleach. This is him." He nodded his head towards where Death watched at the portal, incapable of moving any other part of his body. I looked over my shoulder, running my eyes over Death's form. "Perhaps," I offered, turning my attention back to Lukus.

"But all I ask for is the truth," I said, straightening and crossing my arms over my chest. Arne's face was stoic beside him, betraying no emotion. Lukus called out to him, urging him to do something. As if the god's power was any match for my own. Maybe at one time, it had been. But that was before. Before Death opened my eyes. Before he'd loosed their grip on me and helped me discover my strength. Before they'd taken away my love and trapped him within his realm.

"Alright, fine," I said, raising my hands in a mock show of power.

"No! Wait!" Lukus was too conceited, too concerned about self-preservation to follow Arne's lead till the bitter end. It made it all too easy to pick off those insecurities, to bend him to my will. I tightened the hold of the root around his neck, just as I'd done with Estrid. A tendril branched out, creeping up his face and toying with his lips.

"I'll tell you, I'll tell you everything. Just get that fucking twig away from my tongue." His eyes darted to Estrid's, detached from her body, still entwined in roots.

"Lukus," Arne growled in warning.

"No, fuck this, Arne. She's going to get the truth one way or another."

I raised my chin, signaling him to go on.

"If I tell you the truth..." Lukus bargained. "Will you spare my life?"

I feigned consideration, circling the two beings bound beneath my power. In one swift motion, I freed the dagger sheathed at Arne's side and plunged it into Lukus's chest. Leaning over him, I bent to his ear.

"Your life is meaningless to me, Lukus. I would have never spared you. Just as I would have never believed a word from your lips."

I felt his power surge beneath the dagger, draining as the blade's magic did its job. I pulled the dagger free, letting the now dead deity's body collapse to the ground next to Estrid's.

I turned to Arne. He still refused to take his eyes off whatever invisible spot he was staring at straight ahead, as if their lives had meant just as little to him as they had to me.

"And then there was one."

CHAPTER 23
The Divine

I let the dagger trace over Arne's cheek, down the column of his throat, stopping only when it hovered over his heart.

"Any last words? Perhaps a deathbed confession?"

Arne smirked, not even a drop of fear in those cold eyes. "What's the point in reliving the past, Cailli? You're going to take my life whether I tell you the truth or not. Might as well go out with my dignity."

My lips curled, curses threatening to spill off my tongue. "You have no dignity, Arne. You are nothing. Just a parasite pretending to be a god."

"Tell her, Arne." Death's voice called out behind me. "Tell her how you stole our power, how you saw what we had and couldn't stand not having a taste for yourself."

"It's true." Karmi came forward, her sisters following in her wake. "It's true, Divine. My sisters and I, we've found proof. We've been trying to uncover the truth, trying to find a way to expose them before we said anything."

I tilted my head back at her, taking special care to keep my blade against Arne's throat. "Tell me what you know," I ordered.

Karmi eyed her sisters, hesitant to speak.

"Now!"

I was tired of the lies and the deception. I was tired of feeling like I was missing something or not being sure who I could trust. The time had come for this to end. And I would take down every last one of them if they stood in my way.

Theora stepped forward. "She's right, Your Grace. It is all true. I had my own suspicions about the other deities." Her eyes flicked to where two of them lay, bloodstained in the grass. "I didn't want to come forward until I was certain. I was too scared to face their wrath if they found out before I could break through their hold on you. But there's been a lapse in the records for as long as I can remember. I hadn't a clue what it was until I came across the written record hidden...within Lukus' chambers." She bowed her head, careful to avoid looking at the now dead deity.

"How is that possible?" I barked. "You are our scribes, are you not? It is your duty to record *everything*."

"There's something else." Theora's voice was small, eyes still fixed to the grass below her feet. She produced a piece of parchment from a pocket within her skirts, unfolding it carefully as she handed it over to me. I took it hastily, glancing back at Arne as I tried to make sense of the writing. He gave nothing away as he stared straight ahead.

"It's a ritual, a passing of magic," Theora explained. "Sophia found it buried in one of the old fae kingdoms, one that went extinct when their rulers suddenly disappeared. I sent her there after discovering the lost record, in hopes she'd find something."

Karmi stepped up beside her, laying a hand on her sister's shoulder. "They tricked you, Cailleach. They tricked all of us. They used this to steal parts of your power, of Death's power. They stole what they needed to ascend to the Realm of the Gods and then altered our records to cover their tracks."

Images flashed before my mind. Distant memories buried somewhere deep within me coming forth through the veil of a thick fog. Walks with Death from a time and place of long ago. Massive gardens, bigger than anything I'd created here. Us strolling hand in hand, admiring their beauty, interacting with my creation as they fluttered through the world around us. Enormous feasts thrown by the high-reigning fae to honor us. Festivities we regularly participated in to be close with that world we ruled over.

My eyes found Karmi's, my mind aching as it worked its way through tainted memories. She lifted her chin, pain and rage from centuries of oppression and abuse filling her gaze.

"They used their magic to keep us submissive and keep those memories at bay. They are not deities at all." She fixed her gaze on Arne, a beautiful sort of power filling her features as she faced him, at last. "They never were."

I turned back to Arne, tilting my head as I took him in. Suddenly I saw his face not only before me, but in those memories as well. So similar, yet untouched by true power back then. He'd been nothing more than a fae ruler in the gardens, offering us gifts.

There had been a celebration, something more secluded and private than we'd expected, but we'd made friends with these fae—we'd trusted them. The Fates had been there too, always our shadow, always our scribes to take record.

I looked to where Lukus and Estrid lay sprawled at my feet. Their forms snaked their way into my memories, their faces similar and yet so plain, so weak. They fed us, worshiped us—*all* of us. The Fates hadn't normally been ones to partake in these festivities, but somehow they'd been swept into all the excitement. They said it was an offering. A ritual, yes, but one to show respect and give thanks. Or so we had thought.

I raised my free hand to my mouth, trailing my fingers over my lips and trying with all my might to remember the taste of the food. Perhaps something had felt off, but there was so much merriment, so much camaraderie that I hadn't paid any attention to it.

My gaze slowly found Arne's. His eyes were watchful, his lips ticking up as he observed the memories flooding back to me.

"It was the pomegranate." His voice was low, wicked. "In case you were wondering. The pomegranate was the key, pulling you and Death and the Fates from consciousness. Long enough for us to claim your blood and work our ritual. As long as we kept dosing you, you'd both remain in the dark and we'd retain our power. After that initial dose, it was just a simple matter of destroying the records that proved our guilt."

Horror washed through me as I turned to the sisters beside me, Death close behind. The tart taste of pomegranate filled my senses. Days and nights of shared teapots, of that dreaded pink tea they always insisted on. It was always present, a daily ritual amongst those of us in the palace. Even Death had partaken when he'd joined us for council meetings. All this time, what had the blend been? Rose and raspberry and cherry...and pomegranate. Always pomegranate.

"It was too easy, stealing your power," Arne continued, pulling my attention back to him. "I suppose there's no use continuing the facade. Truthfully, it's always bothered me not being able to gloat about how easy it was to trick you into this fabricated reality. You were supposed to be gods. And yet it cost us *nothing* to perform the ancient fae blood ritual and take that power from you, to alter your memories and keep the truth hidden. As long as we kept dosing you with Lukus's magic, kept feeding you the tea, you never even suspected a thing. You couldn't even *speak* of it to one another, how brilliant that was. The only thing that stood in our way was the other fae rulers discovering what we'd done, the threat of them becoming too powerful and overthrowing our rule."

He was right; it had been too easy. There was opportunity to poison us at every turn. In our younger years we had been too naive, too trusting. But Arne was wrong about one thing: the deities had gotten sloppy, too reliant on Death's conformity. But then he'd started questioning things, spent decades digging through the realms and built a whole library of proof against them. He refused to accept a life without me and kept fighting until he found a way to loosen their hold on us. He escaped their grasp for good and found his way back to me.

"You weren't deserving of the power, of the rule and rank," Arne finished, spitting at my feet as he held his head high.

My lip quivered as I raised the dagger, letting the tip dig into the flesh of his neck. "No, Arne. *You* weren't deserving of it. You took the world I created and burned it to the ground. My creation suffered because of you. My *mate* suffered because of you. You are nothing more than a false god."

I bared my teeth as the blade broke skin, bringing bright red beads of blood to the surface. Arne winced, and I smiled at the sight.

"And I will be sure," I promised, "that the world I rebuild will never know your name."

And with that, I leaned forward, putting my power behind the blade as I let it sink further into his throat. He never took his eyes off me, never tried to fight the weapon. He just let his lips curl up into that sadistic grin, blood weeping from them and staining his teeth.

I tore the dagger through his throat, a crimson spray landing on my face and chest. I turned away as my roots overtook the three corpses, dropping the dagger in the tall grass. The roots showed no mercy, no reverence as they tore into the false gods. No, I realized; it was I who showed no mercy, for the roots were merely an extension of myself—my wants, my desires.

I understood now the connection Death had to his shadows, the feel of that power slipping into the elements he controlled within the realms. It was an extension of his power, of himself. Just as this was an extension of myself. And it felt *so good*. It might have been destruction, but it was a means to an end, a necessary evil to correct the balance of this world. To make way for true Creation. I looked at my palms, taking in every last drop of the power and destruction they had caused. I had no remorse, no regret for what I'd done. I'd righted this wrong. I'd protected my love, my home. At any cost.

My head snapped back to the doorway that still withheld Death. Leaving behind the wreckage of the deities, I ran back to him. Pride beamed from him, even through the murky cover of the portal.

"My goddess," he purred. He laid his hand gently against the barrier. I mirrored his movement, wishing with all of my being that I could feel his touch and not the wards between us. I reached out for Death's shadows, begging them to find me, even here. Maybe there'd be a way to follow them back to the Depths, to break through the wards. In answer, the markings on my palms hummed with Death's magic. A small piece of him forever with me, even apart.

I let my forehead fall against the barrier, aching tears falling down my cheeks. A battle of emotions raged inside me—love and desire and anger and fear. Despite the false gods' deaths, the warding still held, causing panic to overtake me. I wanted him here with me, I wanted to return with him to the Depths. This was our world now, ours to rule and reign and right after all the pain and corruption the others had subjected it to. We were so close to having everything we were supposed to. If we could just get rid of this damned barrier.

"Shhh, goddess," Death lulled as he watched the tears stream down my face. "We will get it all sorted."

I knew without asking that he was within my mind, listening to the cascade of thoughts and questions overcoming me. Suddenly, I realized how tired I was, how drained my fight had left me. I wasn't used to wielding my power in such a way. A sticky spray of red covered my face, my dress, making my body feel suddenly heavy under its weight. My hands shook as they fell to my side.

Another hand laced its fingers through mine as Karmi took a place beside me. "It's alright, Divine. You did well." Her face was a familiar comfort in the aftershock of this battle, and she offered me a kind smile. Her eyes softened as she patted my hand. "You did well," she repeated. "And we will help with the rest." Her eyes slowly turned back to Death, observing the border between us.

I sighed, relieved to be done with it all. With the deception and the lies and the life I was living, in hiding. It would feel good to return to the mortal realm, to help return it to what it once was, to bring down the wards between *all* realms—not just the one to the Depths. As long as we could figure out how they'd manufactured wards strong enough to keep Death out, and why they hadn't broken with their demise.

"Thank you, Karmi." I squeezed her hand still firmly grasped in mine. Turning my eyes back to Death, I raised my free hand to the warding. "Alistair, we'll get you—"

My words cut off on a gurgled cry, a blinding pain bursting from my body. My blood went hot before a ferocious ice chased away the heat. I saw the horror in Death's eyes. I followed their direction, looking down at my own chest to the blade protruding from its center. The blade I'd used to kill the others.

I forced my eyes to drag back up to his, the motion suddenly feeling near impossible. His name escaped me, panic taking root as I searched my mind desperately for it. Everything was so cold. Heavy and cold and distant. I finally found his name within my mind, calling it out again.

"Alistair..."

My voice sounded so distant, so weak. His name was a cry for help, a desperate plea to take away the pain. Except, the pain was gone, now that I thought about it. There was nothing but darkness and ice encroaching as I tried to focus on Death's face. His mouth was moving, his eyes wild. But I couldn't hear what he was saying. Everything had gone so eerily silent.

Then, like a far-off dream, just out of my reach, I could hear his words echoing through my mind.

Stay with me, goddess.

Alistair, I said again, this time within my mind. *We should have lived an eternity together.* I echoed the words I'd shared with him when he'd finally revealed the truth to me. I tried to reach out to him, but my body wouldn't listen—wouldn't move at all. So instead I offered a desperate plea:

Find me in the next one.

His presence grew further distant with my words. I tried to chase it, to run after him and follow his shadows back to his own realm. But nothing was working. My body had gone so cold and still; even within my mind there was nothing but a frosty buzzing, like I'd been walking on too-thin ice and had fallen into the frigid water just below, trapped and frozen in time.

I clung to the sight of him before me, those beautiful black eyes now tear-filled and feral. An eternity existed in that look, a thousand lives and loves and possibilities passed before me as I watched him watch me. It was all I could offer him, all I had left to give. One final look into the eyes of my everything, holding on for him and him alone. He was growing ever distant, but I held on for as long as I could. I clung to him until I had nothing left to cling to and I was surrounded by nothing but darkness.

CHAPTER 24
Death

"CAILLI!" I screamed until my throat was raw, my eyes stuck on the sight of that silver blade sticking out of her chest. Her blood dripped off its tip in slow, torturous drops. The light retreated from her eyes as she stumbled against the barrier and fell to the ground. I was on my knees in an instant, banging against the wards and blasting them with as much magic as I could muster. Her voice slipped into my mind, uttering nothing more than a singular word. My name.

"No, no, no. Goddess, stay with me," I begged. I pushed my shadows out, sending them through every possible opening between realms. Nothing but small wisps found their way through, caressing her as her breathing slowed.

"I'm here, Cailli. I will always be here." Hot, angry tears filled my vision. I swiped them away, bitter that their presence blurred my ability to keep my gaze on her. The pitiful tendril of shadow that was with her splayed over her body, trying to keep her warm. It wasn't enough. It would *never* be enough.

"Fuck!" I screamed, watching as her life slipped through my shadows.

I forced my eyes back up to where she'd once stood. Theora loomed above us, a smug look on her wretched little face.

"What have you done?" I growled.

She leaned over Cailli's body, filling a small vial with her blood, now glowing golden as the last of her light seeped into the ground around her, snuffing out my shadows. I pounded on the wards, letting out a guttural scream.

"WHAT HAVE YOU DONE."

Theora righted herself, ignoring my cries.

"Sister." Karmi's voice whimpered. I cut my glare to her. Her eyes were lined with unshed tears, her face full of shock. She had held Cailli's hand, had pretended to be her friend and earned her trust. She'd given us the book that proved the other deities' deceit, proved who we were truly supposed to be.

"Was this necessary?" Her voice was so quiet, so unsure. I noticed the quiver of her lips, the singular tear that had escaped from her lashes. And it sickened me. "The Divine had accomplished our goal for us. She'd righted the wrong—was planning to restore order."

Theora pinned her sister with a penetrating stare. "She was no less guilty than the rest of them, Karmi."

"This is insanity." Karmi's words were barely a whisper, her voice shaking with grief as she shook her head, unable to take her eyes off the Divine.

Theora's voice rang through the air in reply, power rippling in it:

"This is *justice*."

I growled, unable to control the anger undulating from me. Theora turned, stepping up to the barrier.

"You made us into the perfect weapons, you know," she explained. "You gave us the responsibility of knowledge. Shoving all of the world's—*every* worlds'—wisdom inside our minds, our souls. You thought it nothing, thought *us* nothing. Yet we have simply been biding our time till our power was strong enough to overtake yours. We had knowledge on our side, we had time. All we needed was strength."

Her eyes blazed with insanity, a crazed determination within that only came from centuries of abuse.

"And once I'd learned how the others had been able to steal your power, I thought, why shouldn't my sisters and I get a taste?" She turned her back to me, her eyes falling to where the deities had once stood. "Their power will run through our veins," she said as she produced three more vials, handing one to each sister as she made her way over to their remains. She stooped, collecting Arne's blood before cutting her glance back towards me.

"You may have been gods, but we are the Keepers of Time and Wisdom, the Fates and the Furies. The Three Sisters...and it is our time to reign."

"We were all deceived," I spat bitterly. "Cailli was fixing that. She didn't want to rule how they did! She wanted something different, something better. We both did."

"It's been centuries of negligence, of abuse and indifference for the suffering they caused. Who's to say it would have been any different under her hand? After all she's learned? All you've *taught* her?" Theora turned back to Karmi, lowering her voice. "All of this happened under her watch, when she was meant to lead. And this is how she chose to handle it? She was *weak*. And now she is gone. We can follow through with our plans to fix the realms. This was always *our* plan, Karmi, whether you knew it or not."

My fists clenched, shadows roiling in a violent storm as I rose to my feet, never taking my eyes off the sorry excuse for power before me.

"You will live to regret this," I warned. "I *will* take all of you down for taking her away from me, from the realms."

Theora huffed, squaring her shoulders as she turned to face me once more. "Let loose your idle threats all you want, vermin. The deities have trapped you to the Depths, and I have no plans of ever letting you free. You may have power, but we have all the wisdom of the realms. It's how we pieced together their deception quicker than you, how we were able to find ways to fortify our power while we waited for the right time to reveal itself, how we were able to instruct them to forge magic-embedded weapons with the plan to one day use their own power against them."

She lifted her chin, too haughty or too insane for her own good. "There is power in knowledge and observation. Something none of you deities seem to grasp. You shoved all the world's knowledge within our minds and expected it to not drive us mad. And now..." She gestured to the carnage all around her. "Here we are."

I stood silently before her, letting the mask of Death slip into place as I forced her to challenge me in all my power. If she wanted to go head to head with the merciless Grimm, that's what I'd give her. Gone were the remnants of the male Cailli had helped me become. Gone was the mercy and the justice. All that was left was pure, unchecked rage and bloodlust.

"It may not be today," I said. "It may not be tomorrow. But one day, *Fates*, I will come for you. And when that day comes, I only pray that you've found a way to manifest more power than you currently have. Because you will not stand a chance against the wrath I plan to bring down upon you."

Theora took a step back, grabbing the hand of the sister closest to her. Sophia, if memory served me right. I cocked my head, observing how she pushed the sister behind her, noting the weakness she'd revealed in the movement.

"Come along, Karmi." She reached out a hand for the other sister still lingering beside Cailli. Karmi's face streamed with tears. She hesitated, eyes glued to where Cailli's body lay crumpled in the grass. For a moment, I thought she might fight back, might choose to stay with her friend and betray her sisters. But another moment passed and she retreated to where her sisters stood.

Theora grabbed her hand, refusing to meet my gaze. "We have work to do."

I watched as they retreated to the palace without another word. I memorized their faces, the move of their bodies, the smell of their power. And I marked them with my own, vowing to Cailli on the ground before me—soaked in her own pool of blood—that I would not rest until I found a way to break free and avenge her death.

EPILOGUE
Death

I didn't know how long I stood there, clawing at the border between realms. My throat was raw from screaming, my power drained and my fists bloody as I tried again and again to break through their wards. And all the while, she lay before me—unmoving.

There was no use in fighting, no point in clawing my way back into the Realm of the Gods. She was gone. And nothing I could do would bring her back. She'd needed me, and I could do nothing but stand and watch in horror as they took her from me. Her eyes flashed through my mind, extinguishing beneath the same blade they used on Ballam. My fists landed with a newfound rage against the magic surging before me. Streaks of crimson trickled down the doorway, smeared beneath my hands. I cried out in agony, resting my forehead against the doorway as I tried to catch my breath.

Her glassy, vacant eyes stared back at me. They hadn't even had the decency to close them. They just left her along with the remnants of the other deities, scattered amongst the sweetgrass. Flames devoured the palace behind her, the Fates having set it ablaze some time after they'd left. I hadn't noticed when, hadn't cared to notice anything else than her unseeing eyes, stuck on me as I threw myself against the portal over and over again.

My body collapsed against the doorway, my form sliding down the invisible wards before crumpling into a pile of blood and rage and tears on the floor. She was just before me, close enough to reach out and caress that beautiful ivory skin. Her hair was splayed out around her, a wild mess of blood and dirt. Loose strands stuck to her face. I raised my hand, incapable of fighting the reflex to reach out and tuck the wild tresses behind her ear.

I only got as far as the wards, my fingers falling against the invisible barrier. I flattened my hand, veins flexing as I begged the wards to part for just a moment—just enough to let my hand through, so I could touch her one last time. When they still didn't bend to my will, my hand turned into a fist as I barreled forward yet again, screaming in a fit of rage as I landed blow after blow.

She was gone. I never believed I was truly deserving of her, but she... she deserved the world and the cosmos. She never even had the chance to experience the life we were meant to lead. There was so much more I'd planned to show her, so many more things I wanted her to learn about herself, about her power. But now she was gone, and there was nothing I could do to bring her back.

I stayed with her for a long time. I ordered the Daeomi away when they'd finally come to inquire. They brought me food at first, encouraged me to eat, lingered quietly as they waited for instructions on how to tend to business within the Depths. They were loyal beasts, because I had made them as such. I ordered them all away. Eventually they stopped coming back, and I was left alone with my goddess.

I sat in that library and watched her flesh rot away, her body become nothing more than bones. I sat for decades, centuries, and watched as nature consumed her remains—soil and grass and vines swallowing away the evidence of her existence. I sat until there was nothing left of her to see. She'd been buried by the very creation she'd brought to life. And while I couldn't bring myself to smile, I found it rather beautiful that her creation had taken care of her, in the end.

Part of me went with her. Every day I spent watching her body decompose, I lost a little piece of myself. My mind, my sanity. And when the time had finally come for me to emerge from that room, I left a different being. I was hardened, hopeless.

I wandered the Depths, searching for any piece of her left amongst this realm. My home had become my prison, my being shackled to these stone walls. And if this was my prison then I'd tear it apart in search of any bit of her I could still cling to. I found the night blooms first, their luminance still filling the courtyard. In fact, they'd grown, overtaking the pillars and twining around my obsidian throne. The stone fractured beneath their strength.

I would have laughed at the sight, if I'd been capable of such things anymore. Instead, it brought acid to my lungs. I wanted to tear them apart, shred them until not a single bloom shone with that fucking silvery light. That wasn't me anymore. My light had been extinguished, so why should they be allowed to glow?

But my hands trembled when I tried to reach for them. My shadows slunk away, refusing for quite possibly the first time ever to bend to my will. Whatever deeper, primal part of me existed...it wouldn't allow me to destroy what she'd created for me.

So I moved on, finding her roots, the ones she'd brought into the Depths to tear apart that vile fae male. It had been the one small window my shadows had found her through, to reach her at her end. Their existence tethered the three realms together.

I harnessed them, letting my shadows infuse with the vines as I sent them back up to the mortal realm above. I wasn't sure what I was hoping for. Maybe I thought it would offer a way to break through the wards that had trapped me here. Maybe I just hoped to feel her again, her magic and her presence in my soul.

I spent so many days in that cell, tracing the complex roots with my fingers, letting my shadows snake through them and whisper to me what they saw on the other side. A vast, dark wood, full of watching trees and slinking shadows.

They were my eyes beyond this realm, an anchor to the world I once knew. And I vowed that one day I'd find a way back into that realm, back to the Fates. I knew it might take centuries, millennia, to fight my way back. But they'd made one mistake by leaving me here to rot.

I'd made a habit of waiting over the course of my existence. I'd waited for the Divine to see through the shroud of lies she'd been fed. I waited to piece together the truth behind our purpose and the life we were supposed to have. And now...I'd wait my entire existence to find a way out of this wretched realm. And all the while I'd have my goddess' grave to visit as a reminder of the pain and rage they'd caused me. I couldn't walk the realms anymore, but I wouldn't close that doorway—not fully. No matter how much it pained me to see her, I would leave it open so I'd never forget the blasphemous things they did.

Together, we had been life and death, light and dark. She was my beginning and my ending. But what they didn't understand when they took her from me, when they'd made me watch the light drain from her eyes and her blood pool at my feet, was that she was the one thing that could tame my shadows. She was the one entity that could take my darkness and give me light in return. Without her, there was no more light. Without her, there was no balance. There was nothing—absolutely and unequivocally nothing else that could hold me back or stop me from ripping the Fates apart and devouring them.

One sister at a time.

ACKNOWLEDGEMENTS

Well... that's a wrap on another book. It's crazy to me that I'm still within my debut year and I now have not one but THREE books out in the world. And as proud of myself as I am for making that happen, not a single part of it would have been possible without the help of some very special people who are near and dear to my heart.

As always, I have to start this off by thanking my husband. I've said it before and I'll say it again, he is my rock. My best friend. My safe space. And in the height of my chronic illness diagnosis, he has been beside me every step of the way to offer support and encouragement. He's caught me when I've fallen, he's helped me back up, he's pushed me to keep going. Thank you, my love, for supporting me through another release.

Next I have to thank my alpha readers. I have somehow collected such a wonderful bunch of people for my alpha team. And they probably hate this novella at this point, with how many times I've asked them to read and reread these chapters. But I hope they can still find joy in the pages, because what they helped me create is truly so beautiful. Thank you for all of your sound advice, your amazing suggestions, and for never growing tired of my endless requests (or at least not telling me you do).

I also need to take a moment to shout out the other wonderful authors that are a part of the *From Loathing To Lovers* collection.

K.M. Davidson, C.A. Blooming, Jessa Grey, Joanna McSpadden, and T. M. Mayfield

They have been a constant source of support throughout this process and it's been a privilege to work on this collection with them. They are all such talented authors and I count myself lucky to be included with their names. Each of them have novellas in this collection, releasing between January and June of 2025, so be sure to check out their novellas!

My dream team, the two wonderful people that probably read my work more than any other soul in this world (except maybe me) Sophie & Julia. Thank you AGAIN for editing and proofreading my endless ramblings. Y'all take my creative chaos and make it shine, and I couldn't ask for a better two people to help me prepare books to be released into the world.

And to you, the reader. Thank you so much for reading this little novella. Thank you for taking a chance on my work. Thank you for supporting small time indie authors. Even if my work was not your cup of tea, please continue to do so. Indie authors, no matter who they are, need our support. Keep reading, keep supporting, and keep spreading love and light.

ABOUT THE AUTHOR

Lindsey N. Rhoden is a mom to four crazy kiddos, full-time homeschooler, devoted wife, and a (sometimes more than) part-time writer. Located in the North Texas region, she has spent the last few years as a birth and postpartum doula and photographer, specializing in the art of Ayurvedic and herbal care. She enjoys nature, herbalism, and obviously lots and lots of reading. You can often find her cuddled up at home with a fantasy book, a cup of matcha, and one of her big dogs or her cat by her side. And probably one of her four kids crawling on her.

Lindsey has been a writer from the time she could hold a pen. She dove into the world of literature during college and earned her degree in English with a concentration in literature from the University of Central Florida. Authors such as Ernest Hemingway, Agatha Christie, and Edgar Allen Poe inspired her to continue pursuing her own writing. Motherhood had other plans, though, and she took a long reprieve after graduation in 2018. In 2023, she decided to dive back into the world of writing and found out that apparently she had a lot to say.

To stay up to date on upcoming work from Lindsey N. Rhoden, be sure to follow her on social media @booktrovertbynature or check out her website at www.lindseynrhoden.com

IF YOU ENJOYED DECEPTION, DEATH, AND THE DIVINE...

Be sure to check out the first book in *The Rift Series*

MAGIC MAY BE A GIFT, BUT IT WILL ALWAYS LEAVE A MARK.

Tether Through The Rift is a wonderland-esque, dark fantasy romance about the journey of learning to love and accept oneself. Join Hazel in this harrowing story full of nature-based magic, dark villains, and well hidden secrets lurking in the shadows.

* 9 7 9 8 9 9 0 0 9 6 6 5 3 *